STEP SISTERS

Seán de Gallai

First published in 2016

Do Aoibhinn

Acknowledgments

A big thank you to my editors: Sine Quinn, Bryony Pearce, Robert Doran and especially Ashlene Mcfadden. Andrew Brown for the amazing cover design. My thanks to Sarah Kettles for proof reading. To Holly McAlevey, Kerrie Cullen, Darren McGuire, May O' Boyle Deegan and Dearbhla Lennon for their insights. To my sister Ursula for some excellent last minute intervention. Thanks to Teri and Cameron at Irish Dancing Magazine. I'm very grateful to all my friends and family for supporting me.

Chapter 1

It was the last week before the summer holidays. Tanya and Siobhán lay top to tail on Tanya's bed. Siobhán flicked through the latest Dare to Dance Irish dance magazine; Tanya stared at the ceiling, playing with her blonde hair, so long it almost reached her waist. She groaned loudly. Siobhán gave her a gentle kick.

"Look, Tanya, there's no point in dwelling on this. It's not the end of the world."

"It may as well be," huffed Tanya. "How long will you be gone for?"

"About seven weeks," said Siobhán.

"I'm sure you'll have loads of fun with your Puerto Rican cousins," said Tanya jealously.

"They aren't as much fun as you."

Siobhán jumped up into a standing position on the bed. "Do you want to play blindfold make-up?"

Tanya's eyes lit up. "Followed by blindfold dance-off?"

Siobhán smiled. "Great idea."

Tanya raided her mother's stash of expensive make-up. She made Siobhán sit at her desk before blindfolding herself. Then she did her best to put lipstick, eyeliner, mascara and bronzer in all the right places. Siobhán didn't need make-up—she had inherited her Puerto Rican mother's gorgeous milk-chocolate skin. She couldn't stop giggling as a serious Tanya acted like a professional.

Tanya tore off her blindfold and burst into laughter. Siobhán looked like a stray cat that had been in an accident with a rainbow.

"Ok, my turn now," said Siobhán.

"Nah, I don't wanna play this anymore. Let's play blindfold dance-off now."

"OK," said Siobhán.

"We'd better go into the back garden," said Tanya. "I don't want to knock anything over this time. Remember last time I smashed Mam's vase? She still doesn't know where it's gone."

"Don't forget the iPad," said Siobhán.

Tanya's family lived in a fancy six-bedroom house on leafy Griffith Avenue in Drumcondra. Siobhán helped Tanya to clear a space in the centre of the huge lawn by moving the patio table and deck chairs over to the boundary wall. Then Tanya blindfolded Siobhán. Siobhán hummed the tune of a reel and counted herself in. She jumped around with exaggerated zest, doing her Irish dance moves. Soon she became disorientated and lost her balance. She fell over but continued to hum and stomp her feet. She got up quickly and went immediately into a difficult spin while doing rocks and finally fell into a giggling heap on the grass. She tore off her blindfold to find Tanya in hysterics, pointing the iPad in her face.

Then it was Tanya's turn. "I think I'm going to copy your reel."

"Oh yeah?" said Siobhán.

"Yeah. After all, anything you can do I can do better."

Blindfolded, Tanya hummed aloud the tune of the reel. She started jumping and kicking and rocking and twirling. She tried to imitate Siobhán's steps and soon fell over in a heap. She got up quickly, regained her balance and continued her mock dance. She finished with a bow and took off her blindfold to find herself facing the back wall.

Siobhán had an odd kind of smile on her face.

"What?" said Tanya. "Was it not funny?"

"It was, it was," said Siobhán. "Come here and I'll show you."

The two girls watched the replay of Tanya's dance.

"Seriously Tanya, that was quite good. I'll ask you for the last time. Please come to dance class with me. You have all your mam's talent. It's time you started competing."

"But won't there be other kids there?"

"Yeah, but they're nice kids. They aren't all spawn of Satan, you know. Only one in every hundred kids are big meanies."

"I suppose."

"Think about it. We'd get to dance together in team competitions and go to places like Killarney and Glasgow for weekends. It'd be great craic."

Tanya smiled gently. "I suppose so. I'll think about it."

Chapter 2

Tanya crept into bed and wrapped her sleep mask around her head. She couldn't stop thinking about what Siobhán had said. She really did enjoy dancing, skipping and leaping around, matching her movement to the rhythm. She loved how the adrenaline made her feel powerful. She knew she was quite good at it too—the steps were easy to remember and her legs knew exactly what to do. Everyone said she was like a miniature version of her mam, Andrea, who had been the lead dancer in a famous show called StepAbout many years ago. If she did take up dancing, she could spend lots more time with her best friend. Thinking of this, she became sad. Siobhán was going to New York for the summer, and Tanya didn't have anyone else to hang out with.

Tanya and her parents sat in silence at breakfast the following morning, her father reading the newspaper, her mother reading emails. Tanya lifted a spoonful of cornflakes high into the air and let them splash back into the bowl. Her mother frowned.

"What's the matter, dear?"

"Siobhán wants me to start dance class."

"But sweetheart, I thought that wasn't your thing."

"I'd like to give it another try."

"Do you remember when you were a little girl? We practised for ages and ages and you entered that talent contest and you were very excited?"

Tanya pursed her lips.

"You got so nervous when you went up on stage, you peed your pants and cried. You totally froze. I had to carry you off stage. You weren't yourself for weeks after. You wouldn't even go back to playschool."

"She's a big girl now. She's much more mature," her father interrupted.

"Dad's right," said Tanya. "And anyways, I do love dancing and I know I'm good. I know I'm better than Siobhán, and she's been dancing for years. She's still in Meángrád."

Andrea looked at her husband.

Frank spoke softly. "I don't think there's any harm in letting her give class a go. If it doesn't work out, it's not the end of the world."

"OK, fine," said Andrea. "Try a class and see how you like it. But don't come crying to me when you realise it's not all it's cracked up to be."

Tanya smiled and scampered off.

"You know I always wanted her to follow in my footsteps, but I don't think it's for her. I just don't want her to be scarred again, Frank."

"It's encouragement she needs. You're overthinking it, Andrea. Let her learn for herself. It's probably just another phase, like with the gymnastics. Sooner or later she'll be on to something else."

Chapter 3

Siobhán stood outside the community centre, which was next to the church with the big pyramid roof, near the park. A large lollipop bulged in her cheek, and her lips and tongue were blue from the sugary treat.

Tanya strolled slowly up the street.

"You ready, Eddie?" Siobhán said, grinning.

"I think so. Will there be many others here?"

Siobhán laughed. "A few. Don't worry. They don't bite. Besides, I'll be there to protect you."

Before they entered the community centre, they heard someone shouting.

"Hi? Hello? I know you two. You're Tanya and Siobhán, aren't you?"

It was Christian, a boy from their class. He was eleven years old but already five foot ten and really skinny with a mop of brown hair. His family was from Finland. Christian was born in Ireland, but his English wasn't very good. He walked towards the girls, a dog's leash trailing just behind.

"What are you doing, Christian?" Siobhán asked.

"Oh, just walking my dog."

The girls laughed.

"Eh, you don't have a dog," said Tanya.

"Yes I do. He's just wearing an invisibility cloak. I'll bid you both good day," said Christian with an exaggerated huff, and he continued down the street.

Tanya and Siobhan laughed.

"That boy is weird," said Tanya. She had momentarily forgotten how nervous she was about dance class, but when they entered the hall and she heard the music and thumping feet, her fear returned. She walked behind Siobhán, almost holding on to her T-shirt. To Tanya, it looked like the teacher—a woman with a face full of sharp teeth—was shouting and screaming at hundreds of slave-robot kids. She swallowed hard. The music ended and there was an eerie silence as the children stretched. In fact, there were only ten girls, all smiling. Siobhán tugged Tanya's arm, and she snapped out of her trance.

"Come on, let's get changed. Unless you want to dance in jeans?"

Tanya recognised all the other children from school but had never talked to any of them. They all went to St Anne's in Drumcondra, which had hundreds of pupils and classes. She felt thankful that Siobhán was in her class. Tanya was six months older than Siobhán. Soon she would turn eleven.

Mrs Leonard, the dance teacher, ordered them to warm up. Tanya's tummy was still full of nerves. As she lay on her back to do sit-ups, a surprisingly loud fart escaped. Tanya and Siobhán burst into convulsions of laughter. Mrs Leonard finished the warm-up and shot them both a death stare. Tanya became pale.

"I don't want any messing in my class. Now get into your groups. You? You're new. What's your name?"

"Tanya," she replied timidly.

"Over to the Bungrad group, please."

Siobhán waved sadly at Tanya, who looked tearful.

"Mrs Leonard is scary" said Tanya. Siobhán nodded.

"I heard she goes crazy at Worlds. Don't worry. This bit is just for a half hour. We'll be back together for the céilí team dances after that, OK?"

Tanya trudged across to the other beginners. There were five girls in the group.

"OK, does everyone remember how to do jump-two-threes?" said Mrs Leonard. "Tanya? Do you know them?"

"Yes, I think so."

"OK, off we go."

Mrs Leonard watched for a few minutes, then disappeared back to her senior dancers, but Tanya noticed that the teacher kept looking over at her. Tanya felt awful. When Mrs Leonard came back, Tanya was surprised to see her nod enthusiastically as she danced her steps.

"Good stuff, girls. Now let's try our sidestep."

The sidestep was easy for Tanya. Her mother had shown her when she was little.

Mrs Leonard's face became serious. "Tanya, you're a quick learner. You'll be advancing in no time. Are you any relation to Andrea Armstrong?"

Tanya nodded. "She's my mam."

Mrs Leonard's eyes lit up. "That explains it. Looks like I might have another champion on my hands." She winked.

Tanya felt amazing. She watched Siobhán and the senior dancers practising cool tricks and wished she was in their group. Before long, it was time for the class to practise their eight-hand céilí dance.

Mrs Leonard asked Tanya to join in with Siobhán's team because one of the girls was missing. Siobhán was her partner. The two girls couldn't contain their smiles as they held hands and danced and weaved with the other girls. Tanya was still smiling when the class ended.

"Well?" Siobhán asked.

"It was amazing. I love dancing with you."

"You better catch up quick, then, so we can go to competitions together."

"I will. I promise," said Tanya. She felt confident and determined.

Chapter 4

Tanya sat on her beanbag tapping a notepad with her pencil, her face sour.

Andrea stopped when she saw her. "Tanya, I know you miss Siobhán, but surely you have other friends? Your birthday is in two weeks. Do you want to organise a party and send out invites? I won't have you moping around up here all summer long."

Tanya's eyes lit up. "What if I take up Irish dancing properly? I think I'd like that. Mrs Leonard said I had potential. Maybe I can be as good as you, Mam? If I'm even half as good as you, I'd probably win loads of trophies. That would be so cool," she said smiling.

"Well, I think dance class stops during the summer for a few weeks. Who's going to teach you?"

Tanya stared at her mother intensely.

"No way, José. You can't be serious?"

Tanya's eyes widened. "C'mon, Mam. I'm sure you're just as good a teacher as you are a dancer."

Andrea tutted. "Even if I agreed to such nonsense, where would we practise?"

"What's wrong with the dining room? It's got a wooden floor. It's perfect."

Andrea exhaled dramatically. "OK, on one condition. Let's do a quick trial run. If you aren't willing to learn and work hard and do exactly what I say, you can forget about it."

Tanya clapped her hands excitedly. "Deal!" She extended her hand with a goofy smile on her face.

Tanya helped her mam push the old dining table and chairs up against a wall and raised the window blinds, sending dust particles sailing through the air.

"OK, stand up straight with your arms by your side. Shoulders back. Tuck your chin," said Andrea. She examined Tanya's posture, checking the arch in her back, how far her bum stuck out, how much strain there was on her elbows as she tried to keep her arms by her sides. "Not bad. You're certainly developing a dancer's posture. Now do your over-two-threes as far as the door and back."

Tanya did as she was told. Her mother's face was blank.

"I'll show you a stretch-cut-two-three."

Tanya replicated her mother's moves. Andrea nodded.

Frank stood at the door, a steaming mug of tea in his hands.

"Good to see you girls playing nicely," he said.

"I'm going to get some water, Mam," said Tanya.

Andrea looked at her husband. "Well, Frank, she has all the ingredients. She could be quite the special dancer."

***

On Sunday, Andrea went to Homestore + More while Frank and Tanya emptied out the dining room. They swept the room and painted it her favourite colour, which was orchid. Andrea came home with all sorts of supplies, including marly to lay over the wooden floor.

On Monday, a man came and hung a floor-to-ceiling mirror on the back wall. An electrician came and mounted a TV on the wall and installed a sound system. An exercise bike, foam rollers and stretch bands completed the room. There was even a beautiful view through the French doors into Andrea's rose garden.

Tanya got fitted for a pair of heavy shoes and poms at Fays shoe shop on Dorset Street. She wore the heavy shoes for a few hours every day and rubbed oil into the leather to help break them in. They hurt so much she didn't even want to attempt dancing in them.

Practice began later that week. After work, Andrea made coffee and sent Tanya to warm up on the exercise bike. They spent forty-five minutes working on basic technique. Andrea gradually introduced new material. This continued all summer long, three times a week, although Tanya worked on her steps every day.

By the middle of August, Tanya had made great progress.

"Mrs Leonard called me the other night to let us know dance class is starting up again for the new school year," Andrea told Tanya. "Do you think you might try going by yourself? It'll be just one class. Siobhán is home next week."

Tanya thought about it.

"Come on, Tans, your dancing is great. The other girls will be running scared. You'll be able to show off to them in no time. You'll love it. That's why you'll be lead in *StepAbout* someday. Like I was."

"OK," said Tanya hesitantly.

Tanya spent the whole day before dance class building up her courage by standing in front of the mirror and repeating "I can do this."

Shortly into dance class, Mrs Leonard tapped her on the shoulder.

"Tanya, you've been working hard I see. There's a feis this weekend. It's a pretty big one in Kildare. I have to bring you and show you off," she said with pride.

"Really? Do you think I'm ready?"

"Absolutely."

Tanya was thrilled. She couldn't wait to tell Siobhán.

Chapter 5

Tanya swallowed her dinner almost without chewing. She gulped milk and panted for air.

"Guess what, Mammy? Mrs Leonard wants me to go to my first ever feis."

"That's great, sweetie," said her father.

Tanya stared at her mother, who kept chewing. "Isn't it good, Mam? Aren't you happy for me?"

Andrea snapped out of her daze and forced a smile. "Of course, sweetheart, that's great. I'm delighted. Why do you want to dance?"

"Because I love it."

"Of course. Why else?"

"Because Siobhán will be there."

"Very good. And what might be the best bit?"

"Em, winning?"

Her father grunted.

"Good. Tanya, if you take this up properly, do you promise to work hard enough to become a champion?

There's no point in doing this just for fun, you know? I want you to be able to experience the winning feeling that I experienced when I competed."

Tanya thought for a moment and felt confused. "Yes, Mam. I think I can be a champion."

"Sorted." Andrea smiled at her daughter.

Tanya placed her plate in the dishwasher and then left the kitchen.

Frank spoke softly. "Andrea, you can't worry that Tanya will get hurt in the same way you did."

"She won't. She's got tremendous ability, and I'll keep training her. But she has to be committed. One hundred per cent."

"God, can she not just have fun learning something?"

"You know Tans—she may have the talent but not the mentality for it. If it's not for her, I'd rather we pushed her in the direction of something she'll excel at. But my daughter is prepared for this," she said adamantly. "She'll be champion, without question."

***

Tanya skyped Siobhán after dinner.

"Oh my God, Siobhán, your skin is so dark! Is New York right beside the sun or something?"

Siobhán giggled. "Has it been snowing in Ireland since I left?"

"So guess what! It's happening. It's actually happening. I'm going to my very first feis this Sunday."

"Wow, that's awesome, sista. Wish I could be there too."

"You and me both," said Tanya glumly.

"I dare you to win it for me," said Siobhán

"I'll try," said Tanya.

"Of course you will. Send me a message as soon as it's over."

Tanya lay on her bed, arms behind her head, and smiled as she pictured herself with a gold medal. Her mother noticed the look of wonder on Tanya's face as she passed her door, and she came into the room and sat down beside her.

"You have a weird face," said Andrea.

"Not as weird as yours," said Tanya.

"What's on your mind?"

"Oh, I'm just so excited about the feis and how cool and exciting and nerve-wracking it will be," Tanya jabbered without taking a breath.

Andrea smiled. "You're just like me when I was your age. Did you know, in my time, the younger girls had to compete against the older girls at World Championships? Under 11 was the youngest age. When I danced my first Under 11, I was only eight years old, and you know what? I won!"

"No you didn't!" said Tanya.

Andrea nodded with pride.

"Mammy, Mammy," Tanya squealed suddenly. "I don't have a dress. We'll have to go get a lovely dress before Sunday."

"Eh, no we won't. Beginners have to wear a class dress."

Tanya frowned. "That's stupid. Where will we get a class dress? I don't even know what Mrs Leonard's class dress looks like."

"I'll figure that out tomorrow. Don't worry."

"Won't I need a wig?"

"Yes. Should we look at some online?"

"Def."

They spent the next hour searching for the perfect wig. Tanya chose a shoulder-length blonde wig with tight curls.

"It's gonna look great," she said, grinning.

Chapter 6

Tanya was like a hyperactive puppy the day before the feis. Andrea sat her down with a movie and popcorn in the middle of the day but later found the sitting room empty except for a mess on the sofa. She found Tanya in the utility room walking around in circles talking to herself.

"OK, that's it. Into the dance room with you. You have too much nervous energy. Get on the exercise bike and don't stop pedalling until I say so.

***

Sweat dripped down Siobhán's face onto the sandy brown tiles. The temperature in New York was almost as high as the skyscrapers, and the air conditioning wasn't working. Siobhán's teenage sister Ruth was standing in front of the fan, pressing frozen peas against her forehead. Siobhán went for her third cold shower. Afterwards she checked the clock. It was half past four—9.30 in the evening in Dublin. She decided to skype Tanya.

"So your first ever feis? Excited?" said Siobhán.

Tanya looked blankly at Siobhán. "Say that again. There's a weird noise. I can't hear you."

Siobhán turned to Ruth. "Will you turn that off for a minute, please?"

Ruth grunted. "Fine."

"Much better," said Tanya. "So the feis. I was super excited and nervous earlier on, but now I don't even want to go."

"Don't be silly. You'll love it. Will you text me after every single dance and tell me how they go?"

"OK sista."

"You'll win easy," said Siobhán.

"I wish you were here to go with me."

"I do too. I'm flying home tomorrow, so I'll come straight over to your house on Monday."

"Think about it, Shivs. This is the beginning of it. Soon we'll both be touring the world dancing in

StepAbout. I'll be lead, and you can be understudy. We'll have the best time ever."

"Yeah, that sounds amazing. Hopefully you get off to a good start tomorrow. Bye."

Siobhán smiled at Ruth, but Ruth's face was nasty.

"What? Jeez, I'm sorry. I said it would only be for a minute. You can turn the fan back on."

"Siobhán, what's the matter with you?" said Ruth.

"What you mean? What did I do?"

"Understudy in *StepAbout*?"

"Huh?"

"Tanya said when you're older, she can be lead and you can be understudy?"

"Yeah, and?"

"And you've been dancing for years. She's a beginner."

"Eh?"

"Don't you think maybe you could be lead and Tanya could be the understudy?"

"I suppose," said Siobhán timidly.

"I suppose," Ruth grunted.

**

Tanya went to bed at nine, physically exhausted but with her mind still whirring. She wondered what her first feis would be like. She wondered if the other girls would be bigger and better than her. She wondered what would happen if she made a huge mistake or fell. She had seen loads of videos on YouTube but wondered what it would feel like to dance in a big hall. She pictured herself standing on the podium with her first ever winner's medal. It was after midnight before she nodded off.

The following day, excitement overcame tiredness. Tanya listened to her iPod on the way to the hotel. She loved hip hop. Sassy Miss and Loud no More were her favourites, although she secretly liked The Shams too, even if it wasn't cool to admit you liked a boyband. She sang along silently and bopped her head.

The Minton Hotel in Lucan was a huge castle-like building with its own golf course alongside. There were little lakes and sand dunes within jumping distance of the lobby. Golfers set off to play as Tanya and her mother approached the main entrance. They made their way through reception and headed straight for the bathroom. Andrea attached Tanya's wig properly for the first time. The sweet chemical smell made Tanya light-headed. Andrea added some extra pins to make the wig sit tight, and it stretched the skin on Tanya's forehead. When Tanya saw herself in the mirror, adrenaline coursed through her veins. She felt so excited to finally get to compete.

Andrea explained the procedure as they made their way towards the competition venue. "So I'll have to pay in, but you won't because you're competing. Then you'll queue up to register and get your dance number. I don't think there'll be too many girls in your competition because normally girls give up altogether if they are still in Bungrad at eleven. You're able to dance Ardgrád steps, so these baby reels and jigs will be no problem to you."

"I hate these baby steps, Mam," said Tanya.

"All the more reason for you to win these competitions and move up."

Tanya's breathing became shallow as they entered the foyer. There were hundreds of girls and boys milling around like frenzied animals. Lots of children practised their steps on the carpeted floor, whizzing from one corner to another with great purpose. Everyone seemed to walk with a swagger, head held high, shoulders back.

A baby crawled around unsupervised, and Tanya worried it would get stepped on. Some kids wore sashes and showed off their huge trophies. Others queued at a booth, where a photographer took photos against a navy backdrop. There were half a dozen stalls selling everything from dresses and sparkles to teddies and dance gear. The entire experience was intense. Tanya felt like her breath was choking her, and her head began to hurt. For the first time since she was little, she felt the strangest urge to grab her mother's hand.

"Andrea, Tanya, great to see you. Your first ever feis, eh? This is a big day, isn't it?" Mrs Leonard was suddenly beside them, a programme in her hand, her glasses hanging round her neck. She brushed Tanya's cheek gently and said, "Enjoy yourself, pet. The pressure comes later in the year."

Tanya looked from Mrs Leonard to her mother and forced a smile. Something horrible bubbled quietly in her belly.

Andrea took her to a changing room, and she put on her class dress, which her mother had bought second-hand from the mother of a girl who used to dance for Mrs Leonard a few years before. The dress was maroon on top with a white skirt. It was baggy on her. Tanya looked at herself in the mirror. On the one hand, she had a gorgeous, brand-new wig, the whitest poodle socks and heavy shoes she could almost see her reflection in. On the other hand, she was wearing a raggedy old dress. She grimaced.

Mrs Leonard brought her to a quieter area of the foyer, and Tanya practised her easy reel. She tried to focus, but her senses were overloaded with the sounds of children humming, fluorescent colours and sparkle and hundreds of people. Mrs Leonard didn't look as enthusiastic as she normally did when she watched Tanya dance.

"OK Tanya, that will do. Not to worry. You'll be grand."

Two older girls sat on the floor beside Tanya and retied their shoes.

"Arlene said the stage was so, so slippy, like you may as well have ice skates on," said one to the other.

Tanya groaned.

Mrs Leonard ushered Andrea and Tanya into the hall and showed Tanya where to wait before dancing. Before Tanya went to join the other girls in her group, Mrs Leonard nudged her. "See that girl there? That's Maeve Conway."

Tanya spied a girl with a black wig and lilac dress talking to some adults.

"She's top five in Ireland."

"It won't be long until you're beating her, dear," said Andrea.

Tanya watched Maeve Conway warm up beside her dance teacher and swallowed hard. Maeve practised steps Tanya had never even seen before. She made it all look so easy. Tanya felt light-headed.

"Look how many people have come to see you dance," said Andrea as people made their way into the hall. "Mrs Leonard must have told them how good you are. Are you OK?"

Tanya nodded fretfully. "My legs are a bit wobbly."

"That will go in a minute. Once you're up there, you'll love it. There is no better feeling than dancing and winning."

There were only eight girls in Tanya's competition, and she joined two of them on stage for her first dance. Andrea waved to her from the hall, but Tanya couldn't take her eyes off the adjudicator, whose face was lit up by a lamp on her desk, making her look like an evil monster from another dimension. The light also glistened off a golden bell to the right of her hand.

When the music started, Tanya couldn't stop thinking about all the people watching her, expecting her to dance well. The bright lights hurt her eyes. The sounds of the keyboard echoed around her brain. It was so loud. She couldn't concentrate. She had to dance, but she couldn't get it right.

Tanya barely managed to finish her dance. She ran off stage and wrapped her arms around her mam.

"My God! What happened? What's the matter?"

Tanya sobbed. "I feel sick. I want to go home. Can we go home please?"

Mrs Leonard shrugged and looked puzzled when Andrea looked glumly her way.

"Let's get some fresh air, hmm? It might help clear your head," said Andrea.

They walked along the practice green at the golf course. Tanya took some long slow breaths and soon stopped crying.

"We came all this way, Tanya. See how all these golfers come out and practise their putting here before they go out to play a round? Well, we've come here, and if we're not going to win, we're at least going to get you some experience."

"But Mam, I really feel unwell," said Tanya.

"We'll get you some chocolate. The sugar will help. C'mon, you've to dance your single jig."

The chocolate didn't help. Tanya's stomach felt off, and she couldn't stop shivering. She waited on stage for the music to begin, and it felt like bugs were crawling around her belly. She looked across at the other girls on stage and felt her mouth fill with saliva. Tanya ran off stage as quickly as she could and barely made it into the bathroom before getting sick.

Mrs Leonard found her in a cubicle. "Tanya, don't worry," she said. "It was your first time. That happens to almost everyone. I promise it gets easier."

Tanya didn't reply.

Her mam came and told her to get in the car. On the way home, her mother mumbled about wasting time and money. Tanya felt so ashamed. She had let her mother down after promising she'd work hard, and after all the time she'd spent training her and all the money spent transforming the dance room. And she had let herself down too.

Chapter 7

The following morning, Siobhán called round to Tanya's house and found her curled up on the sofa under a duvet.

"You didn't text me. Did you make a new best friend at the feis or something?" she asked, worried. Tanya sat up, and Siobhán's mouth dropped. "Wow, you look really pale. Are you OK?"

Tanya tried to smile.

Siobhán gave her a big hug.

"I'm OK."

"So, how did it go?"

"Not as I expected," said Tanya. "I felt sick, and I wasn't able to dance properly, so we came home early and Mam sent me straight to bed."

"Oh well, no biggy. It was your first time. Can only get better, sista."

"I suppose." Tanya sighed. She wanted to ask Siobhán something but couldn't.

Siobhán waited, but Tanya remained silent. "What's up? Why aren't you making your chimpanzee noises like normal?"

"I still feel kinda pukey."

"Come on, Tans. Spit it out. I know there's something.

Tanya exhaled.

"Fine." If she couldn't be honest with her best friend, who could she be honest with? "Do you remember your first feis? Did all the people and lights and stuff make you feel kinda funny?"

Siobhán laughed.

Tanya gritted her teeth.

"Don't make fun of me. That's not fair. Forget I even asked," she huffed.

"No, no. I'm not laughing at you. I'm just remembering my first feis. I think I was six, and I was kinda nervous. But all I remember is falling flat on my bum. Another girl tripped over me." Siobhán laughed harder. "We both got in a tangle trying to stand up, and in the end, we both started laughing because it was so ridiculous. I felt like such an eejit, but it was really, really, funny. There weren't that many people at the feis, but everyone was holding their hands over their mouths trying not to laugh. I think Mam still has it on her camera."

"But weren't you annoyed that you didn't win? Weren't you sad? Or embarrassed? I just want to win. Didn't you dare me to win?"

"I'm just der to dance!" said Siobhán with a smile. They laughed heartily. "Honestly Tans, I don't really care about winning. I just love dancing and seeing my friends and overdosing on pizza and coke afterwards. After that epic fail, I didn't feel nervous performing any more. I mean, what could be worse than that? I was able to enjoy dancing."

Tanya laughed, feeling better.

***

Andrea convinced Tanya to try a smaller feis in Clontarf the following week, hoping to ease her gently into competitive dancing. Tanya worked hard at dance class and felt a lot more confident, but the night before she struggled to sleep.

The feis was in a small community centre overlooking Dublin Bay. There were only four girls competing against her, but Tanya's nerves were terrible. She got sick into a bin side stage five minutes before she had to dance and was lucky not to get any on her dress.

Andrea and Mrs Leonard convinced her to go on stage, but before the music began, she ran off stage and headed straight for the bathroom. Andrea found her shivering, her face a pale shade of grey. Neither Andrea nor Mrs Leonard knew what to say or do to console her.

It rained every day the following week. Tanya pottered around the house like a zombie, restless, unable to watch TV or play her computer games.

At dinner, Andrea noticed Tanya playing with her food rather than eating it. "You didn't get much exercise, love. Maybe a bit of a workout would help you relax?"

"Nah."

"Would you like to learn a really cool trick to put into your reel?"

"Mam, I don't want to be a dancer. I want to be an artist," said Tanya, and she made a face out of spaghetti and vegetables.

Andrea's face contorted with horror. "Now Tanya," she said harshly.

Frank gave her foot a little kick and shook his head slowly.

Andrea took a breath. "Don't you like dancing?" she said, her voice softer.

"It's OK, I suppose."

"Well, there's nothing stopping you being an artist and a dancer. And what's more, you're a very good dancer. People would be lucky to have your talent, and God put us all on this earth with different talents so we could use them. Don't you want to make me and Daddy proud?"

Tanya pondered. She loved dancing, the movements, the beats and how her body felt when she danced, how focused she was, but she didn't experience any of those feelings when it came to feiseanna, and she didn't know why. She sighed.

Frank sipped his wine then wiped his mouth. "Tans, you know I don't normally agree with your mother? Well, this time she's a lil, lil bit right. Tell you what—if you give it another few weeks, I'll buy you a bike. How's that?"

Tanya concealed a smile. She had been begging for a bike for Christmas. She gave a loud fake sigh. "Fine. But you better not be lying about the bike."

***

Mrs Leonard came straight over to Tanya at dance class the following week.

"Glad you've decided to stick with it, Tanya. There's a feis next week, but you won't be dancing solo. I need you to help out in the eight-hand céilí dance. Would that be OK?"

They spent most of the dance class working with the céilí team.

The feis was in Finglas that Sunday. Siobhán's mam, Anna Maria, brought the girls.

The eight of them in the team changed into their purple and white class dresses. It was a gorgeous sunny day, so they decided to warm up outside. Tanya felt very nervous and hoped no one noticed. At one point, she accidently went the wrong way and bumped into Siobhán, who fell over. Because they were all in a ring holding hands, Siobhán dragged Jacinta to the ground with her, and in a matter of seconds, the eight girls had toppled over onto the grass like dominos. Blood rushed to Tanya's face as she waited for the girls to shout at her, but to her surprise, they all burst out laughing and couldn't stop as they tried to get back to their feet and wipe the grass from their skirts.

"I'm so sorry, Jacinta," said Tanya.

Jacinta finally found her breath. "Don't worry. It would be some laugh if it happens during the competition. I must tell Mam to record us just in case."

After that, Tanya didn't feel as nervous. All the girls danced magnificently, including Tanya, who danced as well as she knew she could. She loved being able to hold Siobhán's hand. She executed the moves perfectly, and adrenaline pumped through her veins.

Tanya and Siobhán smiled to one another as they took their bow. There had been no pressure; it was all for fun. While they waited for their results, the girls made up a team chant in which half of them beat a rhythm on their thighs as the other girls sang "Drumcondra girls, we're here to stay, all you other girls, get outta our way."

Later that night, Tanya and her mam were talking about the day's events when they were interrupted by Frank. He had a curious look on his face.

"She needs a pony!" he declared.

"Frank? What the heck are you on about this time?" Andrea asked.

Tanya's eyes opened so wide you could practically see the whole of her eyeballs.

"Oh. My. God! Dad, I love you, I love you, I love you!" She ran over to him and hugged him like a python. When she finally let go, he fixed his glasses onto his forehead and folded the newspaper carefully.

"Not a real pony, of course."

"What?" said Tanya.

"Listen carefully."

Andrea placed her empty mug between her knees. Tanya shuffled across the carpet and sat cross-legged in front of her father's recliner.

"Sometimes in horse racing, the best horses get really anxious. These horses are so good that their brains and bodies just whizz—they're hyperactive. And sometimes they use up all their energy or can't think straight when it's time to race. No matter how good they are, they'll have blown the race before running a single yard. So what the trainers sometimes do is find these horses a little friend, like a pony or a donkey, to keep them company in the pen. This helps calm them and distract them from the big race."

"Frank, for goodness sake, where is this going?"

"From what I hear, it sounds like Tanya just needs a little pony to help her relax before going on stage. And that little pony seems to be Siobhán."

Tanya's mum slapped her forehead.

Tanya jumped up on the edge of the couch and pretended to swirl a lasso as if she was a cowboy.

"Bam Bam!" she screamed, shooting her pretend pistols. "Does that mean I get to jump around on Siobhán's back and whip her on the bum and shout giddy up?"

Her father smacked his forehead, and Andrea gave him the oddest look. Frank went into the kitchen, muttering, "I shouldn't have said a thing."

Andrea's face slowly began to change. Her eyes rolled in their sockets, her top lip quivered and her nostrils sucked in air. Finally a smirk appeared. She looked at her daughter for a moment before picking up her phone. "Hi, it's Andrea. I just wanted to congratulate Siobhán. Did you notice how well she danced with Tanya at her side?"

"Ya, it's true she was dancing nice. It's true," said Anna Maria in her broken English.

"Well, having seen the improvement, I think it would be a good idea to bring the girls to every feis together. Siobhán has a great chance of winning now with Tanya there to help her."

"Yes, but I think Siobhán is improving. Only two weeks ago, she did come a second place and the week before a third—"

"Yes, yes," said Andrea impatiently. "But don't you see, this is a turning point. Anna Maria, I'm going to do you a very big favour. I will take the girls to the feis every weekend from now on. You can enjoy your Sundays alone with Daniel."

"My husband's name is Dennis …"

"Yes, of course, him too," said Andrea, not paying attention. "All you have to do is make sure Siobhán's dress and wig and shoes and socks are all nice and packed, and I'll take care of the rest."

"I can do anything else?" Anna Maria asked.

Andrea thought for a moment. "Well, yes. Maybe when they are both in Ardgrád, you can do their tan?"

Anna Maria took an age to respond.

"Si," she said with a sigh.

"Great. Talk to you soon. Bye." Andrea hung up the phone. "Tanya?" she called.

"What?"

"Get your hard shoes. We have work to do."

Chapter 8

That evening Andrea drilled Tanya for an hour in the dance room. "Lift up your feet! Straighten your leg. Jump! Jump, I said. Higher!"

The training continued until the sweat no longer stung Tanya's eyes. She wished she could climb into an ice bath.

"Come on. Don't be such a weakling."

Tanya tried to keep going, but she had to stop.

"OK, take a drink," said Andrea, handing her a beaker of diluted orange. Tanya could hardly swallow air, never mind juice. Her mouth was so dry, the drink tasted like liquid sugar.

"That was pretty much perfect. Do you feel ready for Bungrad solos now?"

Tanya puffed air and nodded enthusiastically.

"You're not to dance another step until Friday, when we'll go over your slip jig. I don't want any mishaps or silly little injuries until we get Sunday out of the way."

Andrea's face was serious. She looked at her daughter, and her mouth softened into a half-smile. She kissed Tanya's forehead. "I'm very proud of you, dear!"

On Sunday morning, before the Coolock feis, Andrea came into Tanya's bedroom.

"I have something for you."

In the palm of her hand was a gold medal, so old it had faded to a caramel colour.

"This is the World Championship medal I won when I was eight. I want you to have it. Remember how special it is to win, and celebrate every success you have."

Tanya took the medal and felt the weight of it, bigger and heavier than a two euro coin. "Thanks, Mam. It's amazing."

Andrea picked up Siobhán first thing that morning. Siobhán sat in the back of the car beside Tanya. The girls smiled at each other without saying a word. After a minute, Tanya handed Siobhán a plastic bag. Tanya pulled out two T-shirts, one black, one white.

"Wow, these are cool," said Siobhán. Both T-shirts said BEST FRIENDS on the front. The back of the white T-shirt had BEST in big writing and the back of the black T-shirt said FRIENDS. Siobhán giggled as she pulled the T-shirt over her top.

Tanya was dancing Under 10 Bungrad, which began at midday. Siobhán was dancing Under 10 Meángrád, which was due to begin at 10 a.m.

With the competition running behind schedule, the organisers were putting pressure on everyone to speed up proceedings. Tanya watched Siobhán's set dance and noticed how much smaller Siobhán was compared to the others. She seemed to lack zip and energy. Tanya then went to the foyer to warm up. Soon Siobhán was by her side.

"You ready, Eddie?" Siobhán asked, trying to smile. She wasn't happy with how she had danced but didn't want Tanya to know she was disappointed. Deep down, Siobhán knew she could dance much better, but for some reason, she kept losing concentration and making silly mistakes.

Tanya kept practising, clicking her feet high up near her face. She forced a smile.

"I'm ready … I think. Just a little bit nervous. I don't really want to dance."

"Of course you do, silly. You're not very good at anything else, so you may as well be a good dancer, huh?"

Tanya stuck out her tongue.

"Don't be nervous, Tans. You're the best by at least a quarter of a billion."

"Just that much?"

Siobhán punched her friend gently on the arm. "OK, this is going to be exciting. Let's go see you kick up sparks!"

Tanya's stomach grumbled.

***

Siobhán accompanied Tanya through the crowds of people until they stood a short distance from the next group of competitors.

"Oh my God, did you see what Mrs Leonard is wearing?" said Siobhán. She noticed that Tanya kept cracking her knuckles and that her face was pale. "I don't think pink suits her too well. If she was wearing white lipstick, she'd look just like a clown."

Tanya looked at Mrs Leonard and laughed. "Yeah, you're totally right."

At that moment, a teenage boy yelled at a little girl behind them. "Sophia, for heaven's sake, you should be ashamed of yourself, dancing like a corpse! You're like a skeleton up there. I'm so embarrassed for you."

The girl couldn't have been older than seven, and she was on the verge of tears. Tanya and Siobhán struggled to contain their laughter. The teenager continued scolding the girl, his face the colour of beetroot.

"You better go. You'll be on in the next few minutes," said Siobhán.

The girls did their special handshake—thumb war, shake, low clap, high clap and wink. Tanya went side stage. At that point, she realised she was gripping her mother's medal. She took a closer look at it and took some deep breaths. She held the medal in her fist as she walked on stage. The same old feelings came back. Her tummy felt sick, and the lights were making her feel dizzy. The intro bars of music played, and she felt so confused that she couldn't remember the opening steps. She glanced towards the stairs she had just walked up. Then she noticed Siobhán standing to the left of the judge. She waved her hands, bopped her shoulders and clucked her head like a chicken. Tanya smiled. Suddenly it felt like the medal in her fist was glowing, giving her magical powers. Her body felt different, almost relaxed. Time seemed to go in slow motion. The girls beside her began to dance, and so did she. It seemed so easy to match the steps to the bars of music. It was like she had all the time in the world to do her moves. And then she was bowing and walking off stage.

"How did that happen?" she said to herself. Tanya looked at the medal, moist from sweat, having been clenched in her fist throughout the dance. She brought it to her lips and gave it a kiss. Her lucky charm.

Siobhán hugged her at the bottom of the steps.

"Did I dance OK?" Tanya asked.

"I dunno. I was too busy doing my own moves!" She clucked her head like a chicken once more, and they both laughed.

Mrs Leonard and Andrea came to congratulate Tanya. When she saw how happy her mother looked, she could have cried.

"OK, it's the single jig next. Looks like they're going to run through all the light shoe dances fast," said Mrs Leonard. "Let's go outside and run through it quickly."

Tanya felt completely relaxed as she did the rest of her dances. She didn't need Siobhán to pull funny faces.

Tanya couldn't believe it when the stage-hand read out the results of all the Bungrad dances. The judge gave her a first in every single dance!

"Tans, love, well done!" her mother said before hugging her. "Well done, pet."

Coming first in all her dances meant Tanya would move up a level to Túsgrád, which was similar material danced at a faster pace. "So this is what it feels like to be a winner," she said, holding a fistful of medals. She felt a little fire glow deep in her stomach.

Anna Maria came to pick up the girls. She had agreed to bring them for milkshakes.

"You were so good," said Siobhán as she buckled her seatbelt. "Now you have the hang of it, you'll be into Meángrád in no time, although I don't think I'd like to dance against you."

"Yeah, I don't think that would be too much fun," Tanya agreed. "Not that you'd stand a chance!"

Anna Maria turned the radio down and listened carefully.

"I wish I was able to get top three or top five. It's been ages since I won a medal," said Siobhán.

"I watched you dance. You start good and then get bad. Maybe if you weren't such a weakling, you'd do better," said Tanya.

Anna Maria slammed on the brakes at a red light and turned round, her face angry like a demon.

"Don't speak to my Siobhán like that, calling her names. That's no nice." The light changed to green and she continued driving. "I don't think we go for a milkshakes now."

"But Mam," whined Siobhán. "She didn't mean it like that."

"I think we better bring Tanya home."

The girls sat quietly in the back of the car for the rest of the journey.

Chapter 9

The girls went to a feis every weekend as Andrea and Mrs Leonard tried to progress Tanya through the grades so she could compete at championship level. Mrs Leonard gave Tanya more complicated material to dance, which excited Tanya.

Frank built a shelving unit in Tanya's bedroom, and Tanya won a new trophy to add to her collection every week.

"Where did you come, Shivs?" Tanya asked after winning her last Túsgrád competition.

"Oh, just tenth."

"Oh boy. At this rate, I'll be dancing in Championship long before you," she said frankly.

Tanya was having the time of her life at dance class and feiseanna. Dance class was especially fun because she and Siobhán competed to make each other laugh while Mrs Leonard was talking. They were lucky that Mrs Leonard had terrible hearing.

One Friday evening, Andrea surprised Tanya. "Did you forget you're dancing your first Meángrád competition this weekend?"

"No," said Tanya, confused.

"You'll need a proper dress. Tomorrow we're going on a trip to Kilkenny."

Tanya hugged her mother tightly.

They stopped off at a bakery on their way and bought tea and muffins to snack on as they headed to the world's leading Irish dance dressmaker—Elite Design. Tanya couldn't stop talking.

"How much can we spend? Siobhán got hers for three hundred euro. Can we spend more than that?"

"Yes."

"The really good ones are two thousand five hundred. Can we get one of those?"

Andrea laughed. "No, sweetie. Do you think I'm made of money?"

Tanya spotted her ideal dress within minutes—a grass-green body with black sleeves and a Celtic design embroidered in white on the front. It was a simple design but Tanya loved how it looked with her blonde wig.

"Oooh, Mam, I love it. Can we buy extra diamantes to make it really sparkly?"

"Anything you want, sweetheart."

"This is going to be so cool. I'll be the nicest-looking girl there. I'll probably win all my Meángrád dances on the first try, won't I, Mam?"

Andrea smiled at her daughter. "I'd safely say so, dear."

***

The next big feis was in Swords. The night before, Anna Maria called to speak to Andrea. "Si, this is about the girl's together," she said getting straight to the point. "I'm not so sure they should be together at the feis. What do you think?"

"Nonsense. I've never seen them so happy. Plus Tanya is progressing with every single feis."

"Si, I know. But that's the problem. My Siobhán now has no medal for almost six last feiseanna. She used to get in top five but now she only get top ten."

Andrea frowned. "Well she is dancing harder material, I've noticed. Maybe she's just getting used to it?"

"Maybe. But maybe we can try them at a different feiseanna and see."

"Nonsense. If anything, that could make matters worse for Siobhán. Let's give it another few weeks." Andrea hung up and frowned.

Preparation was identical for the Swords feis until the girls got to the hall.

"Hey wanna make up some more dance moves for our play?" asked Tanya.

"Not today," said Siobhán. "I have to concentrate on my steps. I'll be back in five minutes. I'm just going to get some fresh air."

Tanya shrugged and went to change into her brand-new dress. Siobhán was the first of the pair to dance and she performed her heavy jig beautifully but came off stage limping slightly.

"Well done, Shivs. That was great."

"Thanks," Siobhán said, wincing. "You have any Deep Heat? It's my calf."

"Check my dress bag," said Tanya

Tanya saw the look of dejection on Siobhán's face after she massaged her leg.

Siobhán shook her head solemnly. "That's my feis over!"

Tanya danced wonderfully that day and came first in her reel, hornpipe and St Patrick's Day set dance. In one fell swoop, she had taken first in all her Meángrád dances, which meant she would now compete at the highest level—Open Competition. Tanya had never felt so confident. Andrea and Mrs Leonard were delighted at her progress and were discussing new steps for her to learn. Tanya couldn't wait to dance in Opens and was confident she would be the winner there too.

Chapter 10

The Emerald feis was the next big competition and was held in Dublin's Carlton Hotel. Andrea insisted that Tanya spend two hours practising after homework every night. On Thursday evening, Tanya stopped abruptly and grabbed her water bottle.

"Come on, back to it, Tans. Sharper turns, move your feet. Quicker!" Andrea barked. Tanya winced.

"Can I just have a little rest, Mam? I'm knackered."

"Nonsense. You're not a weakling. Come on, we have lots to do. This is the big leagues now. Open Championships is a massive step up."

"But Mam," Tanya whined. "My legs are like jelly, and you keep shouting at me. All we've done is dance. I haven't seen Siobhán in yonks. It's not fair."

Andrea's face softened. "Tans, I just want you to be as prepared as possible so you can win the Emerald Feis. I'm only being hard on you because I know you have it in you to be champion. And there's only a few weeks until the All Irelands. If you want Mrs Leonard to take you, you have to do well."

Tanya nodded.

"Do you think Siobhán has it in her? Does she practise as much?"

Tanya shook her head.

"Siobhán doesn't have your natural talent, so she'll never be a winner. And if Anna Maria really cared, she would help her train and get better. But she doesn't."

"I suppose you're right."

"I'm always right. Let's do fifteen more minutes, then we can look online for a tiara to go with your wig."

***

Competing in Ardgrád now meant that Tanya had to wear fake tan, which Andrea applied the night before. Tanya spent an hour rotating in her underwear by the radiator as the tan dried. She felt like kebab meat slowly rotating on a spit.

Traffic was heavy the next morning. Andrea and the girls arrived almost half an hour late, but Andrea seemed to be more nervous than either of the girls.

"Tanya, for heaven's sake, would you wake up? You're like a caterpillar in poms. This is nowhere near good enough. You need to sharpen up quickly, madam. You're not dancing against the likes of Siobhán anymore. These are the big leagues," said Andrea.

Tanya rolled her eyes.

Siobhán's prelim results were called. She had finished seventh.

Andrea scanned the hall for Siobhán but couldn't see her. Andrea became nervous. Tanya's competition was starting shortly in the other function room. She checked everywhere and finally spotted a set of dancer's feet in a cubicle. Andrea knocked gently.

"Siobhán? Siobhán, are you in there?"

"Yes," a voice croaked. Siobhán opened the door slowly. Her face was blotchy with tears.

"Oh, now c'mere, don't cry," said Andrea. "Sweetie, you danced really well. You were just unlucky to be up against some really good dancers today."

"I wish my mam was here," she sobbed.

Andrea sighed and glanced at her watch. Siobhán continued to cry quietly.

"Come on, now, snap out of it. You'll be fine." She pulled Siobhán towards her, and both of them stared into the mirror. "Look at your lovely wig and dress. And look at those lovely green eyes and golden-brown skin. Remember last year they tried to disqualify you because they thought you were wearing fake tan in Meángrád?" said Andrea with a smile. Siobhán sniffled and tried to replicate Andrea's expression. "You wouldn't want your mam to see you with that awful gurn on your face, would you? That might make her sad, and you wouldn't want that, would you?"

Siobhán dabbed her eyes with a tissue.

"You wouldn't want to make your mum feel sad, would you? After all the money she spent on your wig and your dress? She just wants you to enjoy yourself."

Siobhán tried to look at Andrea, but her vision was distorted with tears. Andrea shoved something into her hand. She wiped her eyes with the back of her hand and saw that it was a Toffee Crisp.

"Now eat this and stop crying. I want you to stop crying and cheer up for Tanya. Don't demotivate her with tears." Andrea cupped Siobhán's face with both hands and pulled her cheeks apart, forcing Siobhán's face into a smile. A tear dribbled down Siobhán's cheek.

"Now off you go. She's stretching in the foyer."

Siobhán went in search of her best friend.

"Hey, Shivs, how did you do?" Tanya asked enthusiastically. She stopped dancing and high-fived her buddy.

"No recall. I felt a little muscle pain in my foot, and I just couldn't jump like I wanted to."

"That's too bad. And I'm sure that raggedy old dress won't get you any bonus points," said Tanya.

Siobhán pursed her lips. "What are you working on?" she asked.

"I'm almost finished. Will you see if this is OK?"

Tanya danced a couple of bars of her hornpipe, and Siobhán beamed.

"Nailed it, girlfriend!" she said in an American accent.

The two girls walked into the auditorium and talked about the hot gossip. Cathal from The Shams had started going out with Fionnuala McBride, the lead girl from *StepAbout*, and it was all over Snapchat and Instagram.

Tanya was in a great mood by the time she started dancing. She felt nervous for the shortest amount of time yet and completed all her rounds brilliantly, especially her set dance—the Planxty Davis—which was her favourite dance of all. The pulsing of her blood matched the crashing rhythms she beat into the floor.

She twisted and twirled, leapt higher than ever, trebled faster and turned sharply. Her body told her that everything was perfect—her posture, her elevation, her loose ankles. She spent most of her time centre stage, the judges eyes glued to her, unblinking. She felt powerful.

She was the clear winner of the Emerald Feis. Her face was sore from smiling as Andrea snapped photos of her on the podium with her giant trophy. To cap off a great day, Andrea bought them chicken wings and pizza, BBQ ribs and milkshakes. They ate and drank until they both felt sick.

Andrea kept a watchful eye on Siobhán. Even though she was proud of her daughter, there was something troubling her.

Chapter 11

Andrea was delighted with Tanya's progress. Mrs Leonard added a few intricate tricks to her set dance, and Tanya learned the new moves within a week.

One rainy evening, Andrea waited in the car outside the community centre. Mrs Leonard approached a scarf over her head. The electric windows whirred as the night grew dark.

"Her dancing is as strong as ever. I'm delighted," said Mrs Leonard.

"Great to hear," said Andrea.

Then Mrs Leonard's face became grave. "There is an issue though—Siobhán. She's just not progressing."

Andrea nodded solemnly. "You know how Tanya might react though ..."

"I have to take dancers on merit. I want Tanya to be a champion as much as you, but there would be uproar if Siobhán comes. I'm sorry Andrea—I can't take Siobhán to the All Irelands."

Andrea thought for a moment. "If Siobhán were to win a prelim in the next few weeks, would you reconsider?"

Mrs Leonard laughed but stopped abruptly when she saw the look on Andrea's face. "You're serious?"

Andrea nodded.

"I'll reconsider, but I don't believe in miracles."

But Andrea had to do something, especially with Anna Maria wanting to separate the girls.

The colder October days rolled in. The next day, when Siobhán called around to see Tanya, Andrea seized the opportunity. The girls were recording one another singing with the iPad in the sitting room.

"I heard you're having some trouble with your set dance?" said Andrea.

Siobhán nodded.

"Let me have a look."

"No, Mam. We're playing. Leave us alone," said Tanya.

"It will only take ten minutes. You want Siobhán to get picked for Killarney, don't you?" Andrea said with a knowing look.

Tanya bowed her head. "OK, fine. But don't be long."

Siobhán followed Andrea to the dance room and clumsily danced her set dance, almost tripping herself as she did her rocks. She was frightened of Andrea's frowning face and curved lip, and she stopped mid-step, completely forgetting what came next.

"Look, Siobhán, I know you can dance better than this. Are you afraid of me? Afraid I'll shout at you?"

Siobhán nodded glumly.

"I won't, I promise. I just want to help. Let me tell you a secret. But you have to promise not to tell Tans."

"OK," said Siobhán.

"Turn out your feet."

Siobhán did as she was told.

Andrea put her hand on Siobhán's hip and pointed to her feet. "That's an unbelievable turn out. Your back isn't arched and your bum isn't sticking out. It's much more natural than Tanya's, and it's what every dancer dreams of. So listen to my advice and make the most of it. Deal?" She held her hand out for a high five.

Siobhán smacked Andrea's hand. "Deal!"

Andrea used harsh words to correct Siobhán, but Siobhán wanted to make her proud. Andrea drilled Siobhán on her technique and steps until Siobhán was exhausted. Tanya wanted to watch, but Andrea wouldn't let her into the dance room. Siobhán could barely walk to the car when it was time to go home.

That weekend Siobhán came back to train some more.

"Have you been practising?" Andrea asked as they stepped inside the dance room.

"Well, I don't get much chance at dance class."

Andrea frowned. "Oh, why is that?"

"It's just because Mrs Leonard is so busy."

"I see," said Andrea. "Tell me, what exactly happens at dance class?"

"Well the whole class warms up together. Then Mrs Leonard spends ten minutes with us on our new steps. Then she might send a few of us to teach the little ones the St Patrick's Day. Then Mrs Leonard takes some of the better dancers and work on steps for Worlds."

"Tell me this? Do you have to teach St Patrick's Day?"

Siobhán nodded.

"Does Tanya?"

"No."

"Why not?"

"Usually Mrs Leonard takes Tanya and Colm and two of the Under 16 boys and teaches them new steps."

Andrea handed Siobhán a Capri Sun. "Here, good girl. The final feis before All Irelands is in Leixlip this Sunday. Do you want to give it a shot?"

Siobhán nodded timidly.

"You want to go to the All Irelands with Tanya, don't you? We're going to have a great time in Kerry."

Siobhán nodded with a little more enthusiasm.

"I won't be here on Friday, but I want you to go over all that stuff we practised the last few days. Just practise for an hour on Friday."

"But I don't have anywhere to practise at home."

Andrea thought for a moment. "I have an idea. Wait here."

Chapter 12

Moments later, Andrea came back and handed Siobhán a set of spare keys for the house and told her to let herself in so she could practise in the dance room. The family was going away for the night.

On Friday, Siobhán made the lonely walk up Drumcondra Road, taking a long-cut through the park. She felt like a burglar creeping into Tanya's mansion, her heart racing as she felt a mixture of fear and excitement. It was eerie walking into the dark, silent house. It was normally a noisy house, usually because of Tanya. Her mouth was dry, so she poured a glass of water before heading for the dance room. She skipped for ten minutes to pop music before going over the steps and techniques Andrea had helped her with. She was feeling stronger and more confident and could see the difference in her leaps and spins as she practised in front of the mirror. Time went fast. The clock showed that two hours had passed. She was exhausted. She left a thank you note on the kitchen table and then made her way home, the cold air drying the sweat on her brow.

On Saturday, Siobhán went to Tanya's for a sleepover. They played computer games and watched DVDs until it was very late. When they got into bed and turned off the lights, neither could sleep. Tanya couldn't stop coughing even though she had antibiotics for a chest infection. At 2.00 a.m., Andrea came into the bedroom.

"Tanya, I'll get you some medicine. You're going to keep the entire street awake with your coughing. There's no hope of you dancing tomorrow. Siobhán, come with me."

Siobhán traipsed after Andrea across the landing to the spare bedroom. She turned on a nightlight and flicked a switch on a cable at the side of the bed. "This will be toasty warm in a second. You'll have a bit of peace in here." She smiled softly.

Siobhán was asleep within minutes.

The following morning, Tanya bounded into the spare bedroom like a hyperactive puppy and leapt onto Siobhán's bed.

"Wakey, wakey, sista. It's the big day!"

"Aw, don't tell me it's morning," Siobhán groaned. "This can't be happening."

With a whoosh, Tanya pulled the curtains open and sunlight flooded the bedroom. Siobhán shielded her eyes. She felt like a vampire.

"Mam made French toast with streaky rashers and fresh orange juice. You're so lucky. She only makes that for me once a year."

Siobhán's face lit up. "With maple syrup?"

"With maple syrup!"

"You'll need to eat it all. You'll need all the energy you can get."

Siobhán's face turned into a frown.

"What's up, Shivs? Why you making that ugly face?"

"Well, it's just—it will be weird being at the feis without you."

"What do you mean without me?" asked Tanya.

"Why would you go? You're not dancing?"

"I'm going to cheer you on, ya goon!"

The girls hugged tightly.

But Siobhán looked a little sad as they pulled apart.

"Tanya, there's something I have to tell you. It's a secret, though."

"Go on," said Tanya.

Siobhán scrunched her face and searched her brain for the right words. In the end, she sighed. "You're my best friend," she whispered.

Tanya made a noise. "Meh, tell me something I didn't know. I thought you were going to say you were dying or something."

Siobhán swallowed hard and forced a smile. She really wanted to win and have a chance of getting picked to be brought to All Irelands, but she knew that if it didn't happen, next year would be her year. Everything happened for a reason, just like her mother told her.

When they arrived at the feis, Andrea wouldn't accept anything less than one hundred per cent. As Siobhán tried to focus on her warm-up, Tanya jumped around in her face acting goofy.

Andrea rushed over.

"Tanya!" she scolded.

"Yes, Mam?" said Tanya, acting surprised.

Andrea took a breath, realising she was a touch on edge. "Tanya, I just remembered I left the hair spray in the car. Will you get it, please?"

With Tanya gone, Andrea made Siobhán dance her heavy jig twice before walking her into the auditorium.

"Are you nervous, Siobhán?" she asked.

"Not really." She double-checked her laces were firmly tied.

By the time Tanya got back from the hotel car park, Siobhán had finished dancing her heavy jig. She met her mother and Siobhán by the water cooler. "How did it go?"

Siobhán was still out of breath. Andrea answered for her. "Perfect."

Her light shoe went even better. There weren't many Under 10s there that day, but even so, no one danced as well as Siobhán. Tanya watched Siobhán practise her set dance over and over as Andrea gave advice. Siobhán danced beautifully on stage, nailing some difficult split jumps, birdies and bicycles.

Siobhán's heart fluttered as they sat in the crowd and waited for the results to be called. Time seemed to pass in slow motion as the stage-hand took the microphone and began calling out the scores. Siobhán closed her eyes. All the numbers melted together in her brain. She felt Tanya squeeze her hand tightly, and she opened her eyes and ears at the same time. Tanya's bright eyes gazed into her.

"You won, Siobhán! You won!" Tanya screamed. Siobhán was a preliminary champion. She could hardly believe it. It wasn't until she came down off the podium and Tanya ran across jumping and flailing her arms like a lunatic that it set in she had won. Tanya hugged her tightly. Siobhán admired her trophy and closed her eyes, enjoying the feeling of winning. She wanted that feeling to last forever.

"That was amazing!" said Tanya. "I'm so proud of you!"

"Thanks. You're the best friend a girl could have," said Siobhán.

"Well done, Siobhán. You danced very well. Thankfully there wasn't much in the way of competition. Hopefully Mrs Leonard will take you to All Irelands now."

Siobhán forced a smile.

Tanya was genuinely happy for her friend, but at the same time, she had a strange feeling in her belly. Something was beginning to bother her.

Chapter 13

Andrea came to watch the end of Mrs Leonard's dance class one evening the following week. As the girls got changed, Mrs Leonard strolled across, beaming.

"I've added a few more bits to Tanya's set dance," she said.

"Oh," said Andrea.

"Yes. A gorgeous leap and spin and a few little tricks that I know the judges will love."

"That sounds good. Is she able for them?"

"Of course," said Mrs Leonard.

Andrea helped Tanya practise, but with only two weeks to go before the competition, Andrea had become frustrated.

"You almost have it. Almost but not quite," said Andrea, her face flushed.

"I know, Mam, I know. I'm not stupid. I can see it with my own eyes. Can we stop now? I'm wrecked," Tanya panted.

"You know, I've seen Siobhán perform this move pretty well. We're so close, love. Just another two minutes."

"She danced really nicely, Mam. Do you think she can beat me?"

"Of course not," Andrea said. "But we do need to be perfect. Now up and two and three and four."

Tanya tried again as Andrea hummed the music. She was so close to getting it right. She took a long breath before trying for the last time. She jumped and spun perfectly mid-air while doing the axel with double hop. But as she landed one foot came down a millisecond before the other. Tanya collapsed to the floor.

"Mam, Mam, my ankle!"

Andrea's face dropped as she ran to her daughter's side. Tanya squealed. Andrea helped her into the kitchen and sat her down while she fetched some ice.

Tanya iced it for hours before bedtime, and the following morning, Andrea took her to the SwiftCare clinic for an X-ray. Thankfully it was just a sprain, but the doctor advised Tanya to rest her ankle for four weeks.

"Mam, if I can't dance for four weeks—"

"Baloney!" said Andrea. "I've seen dancers with broken ankles perform on Broadway, for goodness' sake. I know an excellent physio. We just have to ice it for a few days until the swelling goes down. Then we can get you some treatment, OK love?"

Tanya nodded.

It took four days for the swelling to disappear. Tanya had never been to a physio before, and she thought it would just involve a gentle massage. No such luck. The physiotherapist pressed right into the sorest part of her ankle without mercy as he tried to increase blood circulation to the injured area. He manoeuvred her ankle as far left and as far right as it would go. Tears streamed down Tanya's cheeks. During the final few minutes, she lay whimpering, regaining her breath as the physio used the gentle vibrations of the ultrasound machine to help heal the injury. Tanya emerged from the therapy room physically and emotionally exhausted.

"I'm never going back, Mam. Never."

"OK dear," said Andrea as she opened the door to the car, the clunking of Tanya's crutches behind her.

Two days later, Andrea told Tanya they were going to the shops but instead brought her to the physio. Andrea had to hold Tanya on the physio's table as he worked his magic.

"It will be over soon, sweetie, I promise."

Tanya yelped like an injured puppy. "I don't care, Mam. I don't care about stupid dancing. I quit!"

"No you certainly do not!" said Andrea adamantly. "No daughter of mine is quitting."

Tanya refused to speak to her mother on the drive home. Andrea knew she would have to change her approach.

"Now Tanya, I know it's painful, and I know it's awful, but you want to be a winner, don't you?"

Tanya refused to respond.

"In life, you have to work hard to get rewards, and that means making sacrifices. You've heard of no pain, no gain?"

Tanya rolled her eyes.

"When I was in the troupe in *StepAbout*, I wanted nothing more than to be leading lady. I stayed behind after rehearsals every day for an extra hour. I danced until my feet were so badly cut I could barely walk and still went on stage and performed. I asked Boris O'Dowd to help me. I dyed my hair from brown to blonde and cut it shoulder length. After six months hard work, I got my chance. And you know what? All that pain was worth it to be the star of the show."

Tanya was furious with her mother, but Andrea had slipped into a trance.

"Oh, it was … magical. Every week a new city, the best hotels, first class travel. We met celebrities. We danced for the queen of England. We saw the world, went to great parties and got paid for doing it. Tans, there's no beating a standing ovation after dancing your heart out in front of thousands of people." Andrea's face was glowing.

Tanya thought hard. She loved dancing. She loved day-dreaming about winning, that warm comforting feeling she got when she visualised herself on the podium. The real thing was even better. She had won open competitions at smaller feiseanna and loved the feeling. She could only imagine how amazing it would feel to be the best in Ireland or the best in the world. She had to find out.

Tanya hobbled into the kitchen for breakfast the following morning. She poured herself a bowl of muesli.

"There's a physio session booked for today. It will be your last one. I can cancel it if you want?" said Andrea.

Tanya munched her breakfast slowly as Andrea waited for an answer. Finally she swallowed and looked into her mother's bright, blue eyes. "Don't cancel, Mam."

Andrea smiled.

***

Andrea kept Tanya out of school the week before Halloween midterm and allowed her to relax with her leg elevated. Every night before bedtime, Tanya visualised doing her steps perfectly on stage and standing at the top of the podium. On the Wednesday before the competition, she was able to walk without pain for the first time. That Friday, she had a light dance practice, and on Saturday morning, she got out of bed smiling. Her ankle was fine. The rest and exercises had strengthened the ligaments.

As she sat combing knots out of her hair, her mother called her.

"Get your breakfast, dear. I told Anna Maria to drop Siobhán here by 11.30. I want to leave by midday."

Tanya put the brush down and with a flash of panic, remembered she hadn't packed her lucky charm and wasn't sure where she had left it. She found the medal inside a sock in her shoe bag and placed it on her dresser next to her iPod so she wouldn't forget it. She nodded confidently at herself in the mirror and blew herself a kiss. Tomorrow would belong to her. She ran downstairs singing and grabbed her mother and twirled.

"I'm going to win. I'm going win, la la la la. I just know it," she sang, fluttering her eyelashes. She waltzed her mother around the kitchen.

Andrea finished her coffee in the conservatory, watching the wind blow brown leaves around the garden.

"Is Daddy away?"

"Yes, darling." Andrea beckoned Tanya and kissed her on the cheek. "That was from Daddy. He said knock 'em dead tomorrow."

Tanya smiled. She raced into the kitchen, grabbed the phone and skipped her way to the sitting room.

"Hello, is Siobhán there?"

"Yes, she is," said Anna Maria. "But there's something you should know."

Tanya froze. She heard muffled voices on the other end of the phone.

"What do you mean, Anna Maria? Hello?" she said.

Chapter 14

Tanya tried to decipher the whispers. She continued saying hello, but no one answered. Finally a little voice spoke.

"Hello, Tanya?"

"Siobhán, what's going on?"

Andrea entered the room and eyed her daughter with curiosity.

"Siobhán, you sound funny."

"Oh, Tanya, I'm so sick. I was up all night vomiting. It was green and yellow and red and all sorts of colours," she said weakly.

"Are you going to the feis?" said Tanya seriously.

There was a pause. "I can't. I'm too sick. The doctor is coming."

Tanya dropped the phone with a thud on the leather armchair and ran towards her bedroom.

Andrea picked up the phone. "Siobhán, I just overheard. Are you going to the feis? But it's the All Irelands? Put your mother on."

Andrea drummed her fingers on the coffee-table.

"Hello, Anna Maria? But she has to go. Even if she can't dance, she simply has to go!"

Tanya hid inside her giant wardrobe. It couldn't be true. She could feel her eyes and cheeks becoming blotchy. Her phone beeped—a text from Siobhán: *I wish I was able to go with you. You don't need it, but good luck, sista.*

Tanya flung the phone across the room and listened to her mam yelling on the phone.

"Anna Maria, this is preposterous!" Andrea wailed.

There was a short silence before the sound of thudding heels climbed the stairs. Andrea barged into Tanya's bedroom, the door banging against the wall.

"No point crying over spilt milk, Tans."

"But Mam?" Tanya whined.

"For goodness sake, Tanya. You're the best dancer in your age group. Heck, even if you danced Under 14, you'd be the best. Under 16, for that matter! This is baloney! You'll be perfectly fine. Look at me!"

Tanya reluctantly looked at her mother. Andrea's eyes softened, and she smiled, urging Tanya to do the same. Tanya weakly mimicked Andre's expression, and Andrea embraced her warmly.

"See? You are the best. You just have to believe it, sweetheart."

***

Tanya told herself over and over again on the drive to Kerry to be confident and that everything would be all right. Soon she felt better. She felt calm as Andrea helped her put on her wig. Mrs Leonard gave her a pep talk after watching her mark out her steps. Tanya searched and searched for her iPod and could clearly remember the little pink device sitting by her bedside. And then she realised. She slapped her forehead. If she hadn't packed her iPod, she hadn't packed her lucky charm either. She bit her lip, refusing to cry.

She changed into her dress and, feeling lonely, found her mam talking to a group of women.

"Well, isn't that a gorgeous dress," said one of the woman as Tanya joined her mother.

"That's right, Margaret. This is my Tanya. She's dancing wonderfully. Say hello to Margaret."

"Hello!" said Tanya timidly. The other women continued to talk.

Andrea bent down and whispered into Tanya's ear. "Margaret is one of the judges." She winked at her daughter.

Tanya slipped quietly away, dying for someone to talk to. She wished more than ever that Siobhán was there and felt angry she wasn't.

She eyed the children in the foyer. Even though there were at least a million children there, she realised none of them were her friends. The only girl she recognised was Maeve Conway, who passed by carrying her costume bag, and she didn't want to talk to Maeve.

Then Tanya thought she spotted someone she knew from another feis and went to say hello.

"Hi, you're Lucy, aren't you? Do you want to warm up with me?" she asked with pretend confidence.

"My name is Glen. I'm a boy," the child replied, annoyed. "Boys can have long hair too, you know." He stormed away.

Tanya felt lonelier than ever. She warmed up by gently marking through her heavy jig in her socks. When she stretched, she felt a twinge in her calf muscle. She massaged some cooling gel into the muscle and tried to relax by sitting in a corner and sipping water. She thought again about her lucky medal and cursed Siobhán. Everything was falling apart because of her. Siobhán probably wasn't sick at all; she just didn't want Tanya to win because she was jealous that she would never be as good as her. With a mixture of anger and pain, Tanya practised on the marly floor at the back of the foyer. From the mirror by the wall, she could tell that her steps were very good. That was, until she caught another glimpse of Maeve Conway. Maeve rocked up wearing the most amazing new dress. Tanya's dress was nice, but this one was gorgeous. She hated to admit it.

Andrea found her and kissed her on the cheek. "Good luck, dear. Not that you'll need it."

Tanya didn't tell her about her sore leg.

The crushing feeling in her chest returned as she waited side stage to dance. She could hardly breathe.

"Not again," she mumbled anxiously to herself.

***

Tanya's heart pounded as she stood side stage for her heavy jig. She was dancing alongside two girls she had beaten before and tried to remind herself she was much better than both of them. But her belly bubbled like lava.

She tried to dance as normal but something was missing. She missed the feel of the golden medal resting in the palm of her hand when she danced. She knew her feet weren't well turned out and her elevation wasn't as good. It was as if a magnet held her to the ground. She just couldn't break into flight.

Her slip jig didn't go much better.

Andrea and Tanya waited for the recalls to be announced.

"Mam, I don't think I'm going to get recalled."

"Don't be silly, Tans. You were great."

But Tanya was right. She had failed terribly at All Irelands. She was so upset she couldn't even cry. The journey home was silent. They didn't even stop for McDonald's. Andrea listened to Newstalk with the volume extra loud and drove four hours straight until they were back in Drumcondra.

That night, Tanya lay awake, staring for hours at the glow-in-the dark stars on her ceiling. She eventually decided to go downstairs and get a glass of milk. As she reached the stairs, she stopped suddenly. She could hear someone crying in the kitchen. Andrea appeared at the bottom of the stairs before Tanya could hide. She didn't want her mother to know that she had seen her crying. They stared at each other in the half-light.

"I'm just going to the bathroom," Tanya whispered.

Her mother sniffled and wiped her nose on her dressing gown.

"I was thirsty," said Andrea, her voice crackly.

She couldn't understand why her mother had been crying. Did her mother think she was a failure? One thing was for sure: without Siobhán, she was nothing but a coward at feiseanna. A little tear ran down Tanya's cheek. Her sleepless night continued even though the bed was cosy and warm, with her four favourite teddies beside her for company. She was useless at everything, and her mother had completely lost faith in her. And what about Siobhán?

Tanya remembered a night a few weeks earlier. She and Siobhán had hidden under a bundle of laundry and jumped out to scare Anna Maria when she came into the utility room. They had given her such a fright that she'd screamed and cursed in Spanish. The two girls laughed so much, but poor Anna Maria had to make a cup of tea to calm her nerves. The girls giggled as she swayed back and forth, sipping her medicine. This brought a smile to Tanya's teary face. She really missed Siobhán, and more importantly, she really needed her.

Chapter 15

Tanya slept late into the morning, exhausted from having tossed and turned during the night. A gentle knock awakened her. The clock showed 12.10.

"Who is it?"

"It's me," said Siobhán. "Can I come in?"

"No. I don't want to see your warthog face!"

Siobhán stuck her head round the door.

Tanya peeked at Siobhán from the under the covers. "Sit at the end of the bed. I don't want your vomit breath anywhere near me."

Siobhán pretended to hiss at her like a wheezy dragon.

Tanya giggled. Siobhán's smile was something else. Tanya loved her BFF and knew it would always be that way. They would never be apart. "Siobhán, the only thing infectious about you is your smile. It would make anyone happy."

Siobhán didn't feel like smiling. She changed the subject. "I heard it didn't go so well."

"You poop, Siobhán. Why did you have to be sick?"

"I'm really sorry. You know I wanted to be there. But what if I made you sick or got puke all over your wig and dress?"

"Can't have made things any worse! If my calf wasn't so tight, I probably would've finished in the top five. Actually it's a good thing you didn't go. You probably would have been eliminated before dancing even started!"

"Sure. Let's see next time," said Siobhán with a laugh.

***

Andrea pressed the accelerator as the traffic lights turned amber on their way to the Leinster Championships in Malahide. The girls sat in the back of the car, giggling at how red Andrea's face was getting. Icy December air flowed into the car. The laughter died out, and Tanya groaned. She held an ice pack to her shin.

"Why did I have to kick myself? I mean, I didn't even know it was possible."

Siobhán beamed. "Defo gonna beat you now, Tans."

Tanya smirked. "Yeah, right. If I only had one leg, I'd still beat you."

Both girls were quiet for a while as they thought about the challenge ahead. This was the final qualifier for World Championships the following Easter. Tanya wanted to make up for how badly things had gone for her at All Irelands. Siobhán was excited to dance, knowing now what it felt like to win a preliminary championship.

The girls warmed up together but separated afterwards, both serious and determined to focus on practising their steps. Tanya went straight to her dance bag and grabbed hold of her lucky charm. She'd never forget it again. Tanya danced first and performed a very nice heavy jig. But towards the end of her light shoe, her leg started to hurt. Leaping high into the air and quickly bouncing off her toes into her next spins sent pains shooting all along her shin.

Siobhán danced a wonderful slip jig. She seemed almost weightless as she twirled and leapt across stage. The girls sat beside each other in silence as they listened to the recalls, Tanya icing her leg. Siobhán high-fived Tanya when Tanya's number was called. To everyone's surprise, Siobhán's number was also read out. Both girls looked stunned.

"Nice work, BFF," said Tanya.

"Oh my God! We've both been recalled. This is so exciting."

Tanya winced. "It would be lots more exciting if I didn't have to do this," she said as she held the ice pack to her leg.

Tanya struggled to ignore the pain through her set dance. She didn't hold back, hammering the floor with trebles, leaping as high as she could and showing off her tricks with nice footwork and rhythm despite the burning pain in her right leg. Smiling as she finished was almost as hard. Tears were welling in her eyes. Siobhán danced a tight set dance. None of the moves were very complicated, but she had a wonderful presence and she smiled broadly as she danced.

Tanya was proud of her friend. "Oh my God, Siobhán. That was really good," she said.

The girls held hands and kept their eyes on the dropdown scoreboard as one by one the judges' marks were called. There was great applause as Maeve Conway was announced the winner. Tanya and Siobhán made evil eyes as they watched Maeve claim her trophy. Second, third and fourth were called, and to Tanya's surprise and relief, her number was called in fifth. The girls embraced before Tanya went to collect her medal on stage. Siobhán's name was called out in tenth place. She ran up on stage, hand clasped over her mouth. As the stage-hand put the medal around her neck, the announcer spoke to the crowd.

"This girl is particularly lucky today. Because there are seventy competitors, the top ten all qualify for Worlds!"

Siobhán's mouth dropped open. Tanya jumped off her fifth place podium and ran to hug her.

"Worlds, Shivs. We're going to Worlds!"

The girls screamed into each other's faces.

Chapter 16

"Tanya. I have something to tell you. Something terrible—a con-feis-on." said Siobhán a few days later as they sat playing computer games in Tanya's bedroom.

"Oh, you're such a drama queen. Get a grip, will you?" said Tanya.

Siobhán got up and turned the monitor off. "I'm serious. It's going to be hard for us to be best friends ..."

"What? What are you on about?" Tanya saw that Siobhán's face was icy cold. "Oh my God. The sickness. Are you dying?"

"No. Worse again."

Tanya scratched her head, wondering what was worse than dying, and thought Siobhán was playing a trick on her. "What then?"

"We're moving house. We're moving. To Africa."

"Africa?"

Siobhán nodded. "Well, it's actually Ashbourne, but it may as well be Africa!"

"You better be joking," said Tanya firmly.

Siobhán shook her head.

"I can't believe this." Tanya's eyes welled up. "Does that mean you'll be moving school?"

Siobhán nodded sadly.

"And a different dance school too?"

Again Siobhán nodded.

Tanya rolled over on the bed and pulled the blankets over her head. "Just go, Siobhán. I don't want to speak to you right now. You better just go," Tanya whimpered.

"But Tans …"

"Go, I said!"

"I'm so sad too, Tanya. But I promise we can stay best friends. We can skype every night and have sleepovers every weekend, OK?"

Tanya didn't answer. She lay as still as a corpse under the blankets. Finally Siobhán left.

To know that her best friend in the world wasn't going to be around anymore was the saddest thought imaginable for Tanya. It was sadder than anything else, even death.

Chapter 17

Siobhán couldn't understand why Tanya was being so horrible. It wasn't like she could do anything about it. She wanted more than ever for her mam to bring her hot chocolate and tell her everything would be OK. Or for her dad to come and tickle her until she farted, which had happened once before. Her dad had laughed so much that he'd swallowed air down the wrong way and almost died. All the while, Siobhán sat there laughing as his chubby face turned red.

But Siobhán had no one to talk to. Her mam and dad were busy going over important paperwork to do with moving house. She knew she couldn't interrupt them. She knocked on her big sister's bedroom door.

"Go away!" a voice shouted.

Just as Siobhán turned away, Ruth's door opened. She stood there in her pyjamas sniffling, her eyes red, a soggy tissue in her hand. She took one glance at her little sister. "What's wrong with you?"

"I should be asking you that question," said Siobhán. "What happened?"

"Argh!" she grunted. "I don't want to talk about it. Stupid boys! Boys are idiots, that's what. Come in."

Even though Ruth was sixteen, she loved the colour pink, and everything in her room was some shade of pink or red. Siobhán dropped into the cosy cerise beanbag.

"What's up, Shivs?"

"Girls! Or should I say, girl."

"Tanya? Is she being bossy again?"

"I told her we're moving. And instead of being sad, she's being mean."

Ruth nodded. "That's like me and Barry. Even though we don't want to break up, he's being mean to me. I don't think he can handle not hanging out with me anymore, so he's started being mean. Give the big baby a few days and she'll soon change her mind when she misses you."

***

Andrea sat at the end of Tanya's bed for forty-five minutes trying to decipher her words through the sobbing. She eventually calmed down enough to sip hot tea.

"Mam, tell Dad to start looking for a new job. We have to move to Africa."

"Africa?" Andrea chirped.

"Well, Ashbourne. But it's still the same. I need to live beside Siobhán. I go where Siobhán goes."

"Sweetheart, it doesn't work like that. People make new friends all the time as they grow up. It won't be a big deal. And sometimes new friends turn out to be better friends. You'll forget all about Siobhán."

"But Mam, Siobhán is the best friend forever. Do you even know the meaning of best friend forever? The clue is in the name? Forever. Not just a little bit! I mean, is Dad your best friend?"

"Yes, I suppose."

"Well, how would you like it if Dad had a new best friend who was even more fun than you?"

Andrea grunted and stood up. "Well, I hope to God they pull Siobhán out of your school. A clean break is what's best. It's crazy to think that you need Siobhán anyway. Your stupid father put this idea in your head that you need her there, but that's not true. I've seen you dance. What difference does it make if your friend is there or not? You need to believe in yourself."

A sly smile appeared on Andrea's face as she looked at the *StepAbout* poster on Tanya's bedroom wall.

"You'll be just like me, Tans. I promise."

But Tanya didn't care.

Chapter 18

Tanya thought about what her mam had said about a clean break, but it was impossible not to want Siobhán to be her friend. Tanya wasn't sure why she was being horrible to Siobhán. It was all so confusing.

Siobhán came to visit the following week.

"I'm terribly sad too," she said. "But I promise we can stay best friends. We can skype every night and have sleepovers every weekend, OK?"

Tanya swallowed hard, and the girls embraced.

"OK, promise?" said Tanya.

"Promise."

Later that night, Tanya told her mam what was happening.

"You mean she's going to join a different dance school?" said Andrea with fury.

"Yes," said Tanya. "It's so sad."

"It's not sad at all. I just knew it." Andrea's face was all red. "This is for the best. You have to learn how to conquer your demons on your own. Your will must grow." Andrea stared into the distance.

"I wish she was staying," said Tanya.

"Don't you see, Tans? Siobhán is ditching you. She never liked Mrs Leonard and hates the fact that you're the star pupil and she's nowhere near as good as you. Wait 'til you see. She'll join the Montague Academy the first chance she gets, thinking a prestigious school will help her win medals. She's only doing this to make you jealous, Tans."

Tanya withered away towards her bedroom.

***

Anna Maria needed help moving into the new house, so Siobhán's last day in the school in Drumcondra was a week before the Christmas holidays. The teacher moved Tanya next to Christian. Tanya groaned. She would have to listen to his silly stories about dragon-sharks. He spoke very slowly and didn't have the best English. Tanya didn't think he was very smart and blamed his lack of intelligence on an incident in junior infants when he fell and bumped his head.

During lunchtime, Tanya got hit in the face by a ball as she walked around the school yard. Christian was the first there to help her to her feet. The ball left a painful red mark on Tanya's face. She rubbed it and thought about Siobhán and missed her. Normally Siobhán would have been there to help her or, better still, get in the way of the ball.

"Oh no, was it really bad? Who did this to you? Was the ball going fast when it hit you in the face?" Christian asked.

Tanya nodded and whimpered. A small, scruffy-haired sixth-class boy came to collect his ball.

"Did you kick that ball?" Christian asked.

"At least I can kick a ball, lanky," the boy replied.

Christian made fighter-jet noises as he ran in chase. He cornered the boy and grabbed him in a choke-hold. It took four other boys to drag Christian away, but Christian continued to fight for justice. The other boys tried to hold him back, but he was like a caged bear on the loose. One boy struck him in the nose, and ruby-red blood dripped onto his grey school jumper. A teacher came yelling and separated the boys. Tanya spent the rest of the school day sitting on her own. Christian was absent, and Tanya learned why on her way home from school.

Tanya saw Christian and his father sitting outside the principal's office. Christian's father must have been a registered giant, she thought. He was built like a rhinoceros. Christian looked frightened. Tanya felt a little bad but was more concerned about dancing practice with her mam later that day. Tanya couldn't stop thinking about how she had no one left to hang out with.

Tanya struggled during dance practice. She kept mixing up the steps and couldn't execute them properly. Andrea's frown grew more menacing. She clicked her tongue with every mistake Tanya made.

"If you have any inclination to be in *StepAbout*, you'll have to show me something more," said Andrea.

Her mother's phone rang. Andrea stared at it a second and then back at Tanya with fury in her eyes. Finally she answered the phone. Tanya took her chance and legged it upstairs, locking her bedroom door. She took a long, deep breath.

Tanya caught up with Christian on her walk home on the last day of school. He was talking to imaginary friends and pretending to smoke a twig between his lips, puffing white air into the cold December evening. She overtook him.

"Oh, hi Tanya," he said.

Tanya walked a few paces without answering but then felt bad.

"Hi Christian."

"Tanya. Were you crying the other day?"

Tanya was taken aback. "No why would I be? Crying is for babies."

"But wasn't Siobhán your best friend? Aren't you sad she's gone?"

"I hate Siobhán," said Tanya. "She's just a misery guts."

"Misery guts? Oh, that's a funny word. I thought you loved her," he said, laughing. "You always played together."

Tanya felt angry and sad. Everyone believed they should be friends forever, but how could they be if Siobhán lived miles and miles away?

"Oh shut up, Christian. What would you know?"

Christian looked wounded. They walked on in silence.

Soon Christian was smiling again, a glint in his eyes. "Do you like marshmallows on the fire? When you get the stick from the tree, but not the fat one, a skinny one that you stab the marshmallow through the heart first and then stick it the dragon's mouth and eat it when it's soft and black?"

Tanya's heart fluttered. "Don't you ever get sad, Christian?"

"Sometimes, but I don't like that feeling, so I make it go away."

"What makes you sad?"

"Like the other day. When the boy was mean. I like when we are all nice and kind to each other."

"Thanks for sticking up for me. I'm sorry you got in trouble."

"It's OK. See you tomorrow."

"There's no school tomorrow, Christian."

"Oh, what a pleasant surprise." He smiled.

***

Tanya lay about in the sitting room, listless, sometimes in a trance watching television, sometimes colouring in one of her drawings. Andrea checked on her from time to time and didn't dare ask if she wanted to dance.

Tanya didn't even help put the Christmas tree up. Her phone beeped a couple of times a day. Siobhán wanted to skype, but Tanya kept saying maybe later.

Tanya was torn. She wanted so badly to talk to Siobhán but, at the same time, couldn't bear seeing her face.

It snowed. Tanya spent hours staring out at the garden, watching the grass disappear, watching everything become covered in white. The snow was light and fluffy. Tanya liked zoning in on one snowflake at a time, watching it fall from above until the flake reunited with its brothers and sisters. Her father lit a fire in the sitting room to keep her warm as she rested.

Andrea had an idea. The day before Christmas Eve, she knocked gently on Tanya's bedroom door. Tanya rubbed her eyes awake. Her mother's face was a giant grin. She held a wicker basket.

"What's in it? Easter eggs?"

"Come and take a look."

Tanya heard a whimpering sound and quickly hopped out of bed. She clasped her hand to her mouth. Peaking from the basket was the most adorable, whitest, fluffiest Labrador puppy.

"I said I'd never get you a dog, but I know you always wanted one. When I saw him. I just knew you had to have him."

Tanya held the puppy and looked at her mam.

"Look Mam. I know you're trying to make me feel better about Siobhán. But I've figured it out. I think I'm ready to move on with my life. I won't have time to mind a dog. I'll have lots of training to do next year."

"So you want me to take it back?"

"No. I think I know someone who would only love this lil fella."

Tanya and her mother hugged.

Tanya unpacked her school bag and stuffed the pillow cases of her four pillows into it before setting the puppy inside. She closed the zipper most of the way, put the school bag on back-to-front like a baby carrier and left the house. Soon she stood outside 54 Fitzroy Avenue. Christian shot down the stairs like a bowling ball, almost knocking his mother over as he she opened the door.

"Tanya! Oh my God, why are you at my house?" he asked, his eyes wide.

"I got you a present!"

"Oh, I love presents. And Christmas is the perfect time for presents. Is it food?"

Tanya nodded towards the open bag.

"You got me a schoolbag?" Christian said with surprise, his face contorting into a half-smile-half grimace.

"Look inside, Christian."

"I bet it's a bag of food," said Christian glancing at his mother, who replicated Christian's hopeful grin. "Although I hope it's not vegetables."

Christian pulled the zipper a little, and the white puppy stuck out his fuzzy head.

"Oh, holy God," gasped Christian. "It is food!" he added excitedly looking at Tanya, his mother and back at the puppy.

Tanya shook her head slowly. "No Christian, it's not food. You can't eat the puppy."

"Aw, that's too bad. But I do really love it anyway. Can we keep it, Momma?"

His mother dabbed at her watering eyes with a tissue. She ran off and came back seconds later with a bone almost the same size as the puppy and held it under its nose.

"I'll take that as a yes," said Tanya. Christian's mother lifted the little dog out of the bag and held it like a baby, kissing it and speaking Finnish baby-talk to it. She refused to let Christian hold the dog.

"I didn't get you a present," he said frankly.

"Don't worry, Christian, that's OK."

"Actually I think it's unfair that you gave me a present without telling me so as I could get you something. But never mind, I really love her. I'm going to call her Tanya Junior."

"It's a boy," said Tanya.

"Puppies can be boys?"

"Yes, Christian."

"Oh. In that case, I'll call him Barky."

Tanya squished her face and glanced at the happy puppy. "OK, I'd better go."

Chapter 19

Tanya felt focused after Christmas. The next feis was a small event at the Crown Plaza in Northwood. Andrea couldn't take Tanya because she had to work on Sunday, and her father was in Cardiff on business, so Grandad Dermot had to take her to the feis.

Grandad Dermot was a funny old man. He didn't know a thing about Irish dancing and also despised children apart from Tanya.

"So what is this emergency? Tonsillitis? Appendicitis, epiglottitis?" said Grandad Dermot as Tanya got into his battered old car. Despite being rich, Dermot refused to replace his banger because, he said, the engine worked like a charm.

"No, Grandad." Tanya giggled. "I have a dance competition."

"Oh, I see. What are the symptoms? Bad breath? Hunchback? Diarrhoea?"

"No. it's a feis. Irish dancing."

"Irish dancing?!" he yelled and pretended to slam on the brakes. "Oh angels in heaven, bring me to my grave. With kids? More of them? All ... like you?" He eyed her suspiciously.

Tanya tried not to giggle. "Hundreds of them."

They drove without talking for a while. Between the old-car smell and classical music, Tanya felt very sophisticated. She melted into the big leather seats.

Tanya got warmed up and changed with Mrs Leonard's help.

"How have you been performing?" Grandad asked.

"Oh, I dunno. I only seem to do well when Siobhán is here. She was my lucky charm. But she moved away. I'll be lucky to finish last."

"I remember her. She was a lovely girl. I bet you miss her a lot?"

"No, I hate her."

"Hate? My gosh. But she was your best friend. Do you mean to tell me you hate her because she's not living round the corner anymore?"

Tanya didn't answer.

"Dear oh dear, Tanya. Tut tut. And you know, there's no such thing as a good-luck charm—it's all up here," he said, tapping his bald head. "As a wise man once said, if you think you can or think you can't, you're probably right. The most important thing is to do it because you love it and it's fun. The rest will come. Now get up there and perform. And pretend the audience are all wearing clown clothes."

Tanya giggled. He kissed her on the forehead.

Tanya went to her dance bag and found her mother's gold medal.

"Maybe Grandad's right," she said quietly. "Maybe I don't need you or Siobhán." She tucked the medal into her spare socks and zipped her bag.

Tanya warmed up and went side stage with Grandad's words ringing in her ears. All she had to do was enjoy dancing.

She danced against girls she had beaten before, and when she got nervous, she reminded herself of what

Grandad had said. The result didn't really matter. She'd come off stage and still be alive and still be eleven and still have her whole life ahead of her to enjoy. Tanya danced her best. She knew she hadn't quite hit all her marks. Her heavy jig didn't go so well, but her slip jig and set dance went a little better, but she didn't get placed. Grandpa treated her to a salmon and broccoli quiche at a nearby café afterwards, and Siobhán felt pleased with how things had gone.

On the way home, Andrea called Grandad Dermot's phone.

"Hi, put Tanya on, please. How did you do, sweetheart?"

"Meh, I did OK. Not bad, like. I think I danced nicely, but I didn't get a place."

"I see," said Andrea.

"Mam, can we go to the Derry feis in a few weeks? It will be cool to go, won't it?"

"We'll see," said Andrea. "I'll talk to you later."

Tanya sat back and relaxed. She hadn't won, but she'd had fun. She wondered how Siobhán was doing. Maybe it was time to send her a message.

Chapter 20

Siobhán's family moved into their new house during Christmas week. Siobhán couldn't get comfortable no matter what room she sat in—everything was just too foreign. Ruth never sat in the sitting room anymore, having fallen in love with her new giant bedroom.

Tanya needed to talk to someone. Her mam was busy cooking dinner. She told her to talk to her father, who wasn't even home. Siobhán began to see just how difficult the change was. She dreaded to think how hard it would be to start at a new school and make new friends. She worried about this all through the Christmas holidays and felt miserable.

Siobhán kept her head down on the first day at her new school. It was nerve-wracking—just a gazillion faces and a bazillion names. That same week, she went to her new Irish dance school, which was the big rival to her old school in Drumcondra.

The dance school in Ashbourne was a modern building that didn't make you sneeze as much as the hall in Drumcondra. Everything seemed bigger, brighter and better. She arrived twenty minutes early, nervous of making a bad impression and being disliked. She was from the enemy school, so they had every reason to hate her.

Miss Montague, the dance teacher, greeted her at the door with a huge smile.

"Hi Siobhán. You're going to love it here. We all love dancing at this school, and having fun," she said. She was a tall, slim, sharp-faced woman with shoulder-length auburn hair. But her smile was tender. Mrs Montague asked if Siobhán and the other early-comers would help the younger dancers.

One of the girls came over to her immediately. "Hi, are you Siobhán? I'm Nicole. I'm so glad you joined. Megan hurt her ankle, so we need one more for the eight-hand céilí."

Siobhán felt relaxed immediately.

The class went well. After regular class ended, they stayed behind for another half hour to work on the eight-hand céilí dance. Siobhán knew it already, so it was just a matter of going over it a few times. Miss Montague was very helpful in spotting some basic errors that Siobhán was making and helped correct them. This made Siobhán feel great.

The following weekend, Siobhán danced with her new céilí team, and they came first. Her confidence was higher than ever.

Weeks of dance class went by. Siobhán worked hard on strengthening exercises that the teacher gave her to help her elevation and technique. The teacher's daughter, Mairéad, stayed back with Siobhán for a half hour after class for two weeks, teaching her a new step. One day after class, as Siobhán got ready to leave, Miss Montague called her over.

"Siobhán, come here a moment."

Siobhán felt nervous. Maybe she wasn't up to the standard required at the Montague Academy. After all, they only ever had champion dancers. She swallowed hard and went over to Miss Montague. Her face was very serious.

"Mairéad tells me she's been spending extra time with you."

"Yes, Miss Montague," said Siobhán shyly.

"She's been doing this for the past four weeks out of the goodness of her heart."

Siobhán felt like her own heart would burst.

"You've only danced in a couple of team dances, but Mairéad has informed me—" At that moment she broke into a fit of coughing, and Siobhán waited anxiously. "She has informed me that she thinks you're ready to dance in solos."

Siobhán couldn't believe her ears.

Chapter 21

Christian was turning out to be a great friend to Tanya, and she helped him with his school work. He was a lot calmer with her around. The teacher rewarded them with homework passes three weeks in a row.

In the yard, they drew pictures of dinosaurs from outer space and played with fantasy game cards. When Tanya went to Christian's house, they played Galactica—an online game Tanya never thought she'd like but quickly became addicted to. The littlest things amazed Christian, and his reactions made Tanya laugh. But he wasn't Siobhán. Sometimes Tanya looked at photographs of her and Siobhán on Instagram. Sometimes she cried with laughter, sometimes in sadness. Other times, she felt so angry she wanted to delete all photos of the two of them together.

Siobhán's eleventh birthday was coming up. Tanya had thought about messaging her but couldn't bring herself to, despite what Grandad Dermot had said.

Siobhán sent birthday party invites out for that coming Friday. Tanya wasn't sure what to do.

"I'm not going, and if I was, I wouldn't go on Friday. All her stupid new friends who I don't even know will be there."

"I have a great idea," said Christian. His face lit up as if a cartoon light bulb shone above his head. "Why don't you go on Saturday? We can make her a present and deliver it to her personally. That would be really cool. She will really like that."

"No, Christian, this is your stupidest idea yet!"

"Think about it. If you make friends with her again, you can have your best friend back in your life, and that will mean you will have two best friends." He smiled, but his smile looked more like a grimace. "Think about it. You are not the evil one. She is the evil one who moved to a foreign country and deserted you in the wilderness forever. But if you make the peace offering, you can end up looking like the supreme leader and be forever happy too."

Tanya thought in silence.

"If I show up at her house with a peace offering, she might forget that it was me that was mean to her in the first place."

She turned to Christian. "Christian, I think we should take the initiative and bring a present to Siobhán's new house for her birthday."

Christian's mouth dropped open. "But, but that's what I was—"

"Enough jabbering, boy. Now, what to get her?"

"We will make a life-sized pterodactyl out of cereal boxes. I shall wear my dad's jumpsuit for the painting of exhibit A."

"Agreed," said Tanya, extending her arm in handshake.

She went into town with her mother during the week and bought another present for Siobhán—a new sports bag for her dance gear.

Tanya bit her fingernails, playing out every possible scenario in her mind, wondering how Siobhán would react when she showed up at her house. The best version ended with the two of them slurping ice cream. A less fortunate ending was one where Tanya smashed an ice cream cone in Siobhán's face and ran home. The worst possible scenario, which she tried not to think about, involved a fire-brigade, four police cars, an ambulance and Tanya stealing a car. There was always the possibility that Siobhán wouldn't be home, and part of her hoped that would be the case.

That Saturday, Christian met her at the bus stop near the bank. He wore a bigger-than-usual smile, which matched the face of the massive grey pterodactyl model he was carrying.

"Wow, this is really exciting, isn't it? Going on the bus!"

"Christian? Really? Have you never been on the bus before?"

"Yeah," he said with wide eyes. "I like to sit up the stairs. It's like being a giant, and all the people are so small, and you can crush them if you want." He made mechanical stomping sounds.

"I had to be very careful sneaking out. If Mam knew I was going on the bus by myself, she'd have a fit," said Tanya.

"But you're not going on the bus by your own self," said Christian, eyes popping.

"I know, Christian, I know. You're coming with me! If I told Mam that, it would've made it worse, trust me."

Christian blinked in confusion.

"What did you tell your parents?" Tanya asked.

"I said I was going on a bus adventure, and my mam gave me these." He proudly held up a giant bag of jellies.

After ten minutes, their bus came, and off they went on the forty-five minute journey to Ashbourne. When they got there, Tanya used Google Maps on her phone to guide them towards Siobhán's house.

Tanya had pains in her stomach as they walked through the estate towards number 42. It was an end-ofterrace house and had a garden at the front. It was a mansion compared to their other house. There was a big green separating the two sides of the estate. Christian saw swings and slides in a play area.

"Oh, look. Park toys! Look at the ladders and everything coming out from the ground," he said.

This was a good thing, Tanya thought. "Hey Christian, why don't you go and play there for a few minutes? I'll get Siobhán, and then we'll go over."

"Like a play date? Oh, that will be fun! OK, but first, hold this," he said, handing Tanya the pterodactyl. Off he went, running as fast as his gangly legs could carry him.

It took Tanya a few minutes to knock on the door. Her belly was doing jumping jacks. What if Siobhán didn't want to talk to her and slammed the door in her face? In a way, she couldn't blame her if she did. Tanya had been horrible to her. It all became clear to her as she stood staring at the golden number 42 on the big red door. Finally she knocked. Nothing happened. She rang the doorbell. She heard footsteps running down the stairs. Siobhán opened the door and clasped both her hands over her mouth, looking in bemusement first at Siobhán and then at the pterodactyl.

"Oh my God! What are you doing here?"

Tanya waited anxiously. Finally Siobhán's face broke into a giant smile. She grabbed Tanya and hugged her tightly.

"Come in, come in. See my new casa," said Siobhán.

Tanya's heart thumped through her chest, and a great sense of relief swept through her body. She couldn't stop smiling. They went upstairs, nattering like they used to. Everything felt so normal. Siobhán loved the present. All of a sudden, they heard a thumping on the door. Siobhán face filled with concern.

Tanya jumped up. "Oh God, I forgot all about Christian."

"Christian?" said Siobhán.

Tanya raced downstairs.

Christian was standing at the door panting. "Tanya, this big dog started chasing me, and it was trying to bite my legs off, and I was really scared."

Tanya looked over his shoulder as Siobhán joined her.

"Oh no, he's coming again," said Christian as he pushed his way inside.

Tanya and Siobhán burst out laughing when they saw Christian's vicious attacker—a tiny white fluff ball running after a ball.

"Look at him. It's so evil! If Barky was here, he would protect me, but he's not. I need protection," Christian squealed. He headed straight for the fridge and took out a packet of ham.

"So are you friends again?" asked Christian, munching.

The two girls looked at each other and smiled.

"Yes," they said triumphantly.

After a tour of the house, they made popcorn and went to Siobhán's bedroom to play. Tanya hadn't laughed as much in weeks. Everything Christian said and did had the girls in stitches.

"Are you still dancing?" asked Siobhán.

Tanya felt awkward answering.

"Yes. I'm doing OK. Getting better all the time, I think."

"Look, I have to show you my birthday present," said Siobhán. "It was a total surprise. Mam and Dad were saving for ages."

Siobhán opened the wardrobe and pulled out a dress bag. She unzipped it and took out a brand-new Irish dance dress. Tanya stopped breathing.

"Wow, it's nice! Well done, Siobhán," she said calmly. "You must be very happy with it."

"I absolutely adore it," said Siobhán, beaming.

Tanya continued smiling, but her heart had stopped beating. The dress was from Elite Design. It was the most gorgeous dress she had ever seen, fabulous gold and silver Celtic designs on the whitest material. She could hardly comprehend what was happening as Siobhán kept jabbering.

"And my new dance teacher is bringing me to my first major tomorrow and says I should do well. It's the Derry feis. I just feel like the steps are starting to make sense in my brain now."

Tanya had wanted to go to the Derry feis, but because she hadn't even placed in her last feis, Andrea was unwilling to travel the long distance. Tanya learned that Siobhán was now dancing for the Montague Academy. Tanya's head was a muddle.

She checked the time on her phone and announced dramatically, "Oh God, look at the time. Christian, we should really go before it gets dark."

Siobhán's face dropped. "Are you sure? But it's still only early. I have chocolate cake."

"Oh, I love chocolate, especially when it's inside cake," said Christian, rubbing his hands together.

"No really, we should go," said Tanya, standing up. Christian insisted they all hug goodbye, and soon they were walking towards the bus stop.

"Isn't it weird how when you have a best friend, sometimes you have a fall out, but no matter what, you always end up friends again because that's what best friends forever really means? Isn't that weird?" said Christian.

"Isn't it just," said Tanya.

Chapter 22

That Monday, Tanya sat on a high stool at the breakfast bar and looked up the Derry feis results on her iPad. Even though Siobhán hadn't placed top ten overall, she had come sixth in her hornpipe. Tanya felt strange. Had the new dress helped Siobhán catch the judge's attention? Or was she improving at her new school?

Tanya kept in mind the positives from the Northwood feis when she went to her next feis in Dundrum.

She felt calm and warmed up well, satisfied that she was hitting the mark in all her steps. Just as she finished, someone shouted her name.

"Tanya! How did I not see you?"

A girl wearing a gorgeous white dress came across. It was Siobhán. She was wearing a black Penelope wig, and her face was made up beautifully, her legs perfectly tanned. She looked gorgeous as she bounced towards Tanya.

"Oh, I didn't expect you to be here," said Tanya.

"My teacher thought I was very unlucky at the Derry feis, so she wanted me to try again. Did I tell you I finished sixth in my hornpipe? It was so exciting."

"Oh, maybe I can help you a bit?" said Tanya. "Are you doing the Planxty Davis?"

"No. We do The Vanishing Lake in our school."

"Oh, I don't know that one," said Tanya.

"It's really nice. Look."

Siobhán danced a few steps, humming loudly. It was a really nice step, and Tanya was surprised at how well Siobhán danced. Her rhythm and footwork had improved so much.

Then Andrea arrived and grabbed Tanya by the shoulders. "You can talk to your friend after. You're on soon. Come on, Tanya."

Tanya felt rushed after that, and her head was filled with clouds. She didn't begin her step in time with the music, and her confidence seemed to evaporate in the sweltering hot hall. She could barely focus on her steps and was glad when it was over. As the competition went on, Tanya found it harder and harder to execute the more complicated steps. She couldn't do them with any fluidity.

After dancing, Tanya joined her mother. "Mam, my ankle is really sore. I don't think I should dance anymore."

Andrea was silent for a moment. "Go and ice it for a minute. I need a quick word with your teacher."

Mrs Leonard's face was glum. "She's not putting the effort in."

Andrea scratched her chin. "She's complaining about her ankle."

Mrs Leonard shook her head in disappointment.

"That ankle business is all in her head. She'll have to learn to get over those little niggles. I need her to start acting like a champion." Andrea bit her bottom lip. "And what exactly did you do to Siobhán McMahon? She never showed me any ability at class."

Andrea looked back at her in surprise.

"I don't think she should continue today." said Andrea'

"What?" said Mrs Leonard in surprise. "She has to get back up on that stage."

"I'd rather not risk her ankle," said Andrea.

Mrs Leonard shrugged. "Fine. Suit yourself."

Andrea went in search of her daughter.

"OK Tanya, get changed. That's enough for one day."

Later that evening Siobhán texted Tanya: *Sorry I didn't get to say goodbye. Hard luck today. You'll never guess where I came!*

Tanya threw the phone onto her lap. She didn't feel well that night.

Chapter 23

Siobhán baked cupcakes to thank Tanya for the birthday gift, and she visited her in Drumcondra. Tanya was still surprised and jealous that Siobhán had placed eighth at the feis. The girls sat in the kitchen eating.

"My dance teacher wants me to start learning the Planxty Davis set dance soon," said Siobhán.

"Really? That's a super long set dance. You might not have the stamina for it, Siobhán."

"Well, my teacher thinks I might be ready."

"I think you should go easy," said Tanya with a sad smile. "I don't think you train as much as me or have the natural ability."

Siobhán was hurt. "But I am growing and getting stronger. I think I'm getting better, and all I have to do is keep dancing."

"Don't rush it, though. You'll only be disappointed."

Siobhán's enthusiastic manner changed. "Maybe you're right. I might never be good enough."

Tanya nodded her head in agreement. "I just don't want you to get your hopes up and be disappointed. When it comes to competing in the All Irelands and Worlds, it's really tough. You probably wouldn't get a recall." Tanya gave an evil smile. "On the plus side, though, you'd be there to cheer me on when I win. Wouldn't that be fun?"

Siobhán glared at Tanya. "That's what you actually think? You've always thought you were better than me at everything, Tanya. You've always made me feel small. You don't want me to do well."

Tanya thought of everything her mam had said about why Siobhán really moved dance school. "That's not true. I do want you to do well. You don't actually think you could beat me, though, do you?"

"Well, I beat you on Sunday. I placed eighth, didn't I?"

"That's only because I got injured."

"I hate you, Tanya," Siobhán yelled. "Moving away was the best thing that has ever happened. I never want to speak to you again. You're the worst friend a person could have."

Tanya was unable to control her temper.

"You witch, Siobhán. My mam was right all along. You've always been jealous of me being a better dancer than you, and you jumping ship to go to the Montague Academy proves it. You've always wanted to ditch me."

Siobhán almost fell over in shock, but Tanya didn't let her get a word in.

"Then you go and buy a new dress, more expensive than mine, to show off and rub it in my face. You can't buy medals, Siobhán, and you can't buy talent. There isn't enough money in the world that could help you beat me."

Siobhán stormed out the front door. Her mam wasn't due to pick her up for another hour. She wandered around Griffith Park as she waited to be collected.

Tanya picked up the phone and called Christian.

"Are you crying? It sounds like there's tears coming out of your eyes on the other end of the phone. Did someone die?"

"Yes, Christian, more or less. Siobhán. She's dead to me!"

Christian visited later that evening. They stood in the back garden as the rain poured down. Christian looked very sad. He was wearing Tanya's father's rain coat and held the shaft of a shovel. They both stooped over a freshly dug hole. Tanya, dressed in black, a deep frown on her wet face, threw jewellery, teddies and books—anything associated with Siobhán—into the hole. The paper crinkled loudly in the rain. Christian shook his head gravely as he watched the items fall into the mucky tomb.

"Oh my, oh my. This really is serious, isn't it?"

Tanya demanded the shovel and scooped earth into the hole and patted it down neatly. They went back inside, leaving muddy footprints behind them.

When Christian went home, Tanya stayed in her father's study, plotting. After some time, she searched out her mother and handed her a piece of paper.

"Mam, here are the upcoming feises before Worlds. I have to win. We might have to take some time off. There's a camp rince in Berlin on the 25th of January I think we should go to. Glen Dunne is giving it. Next week, there's a feis in Donegal. I think we should go to that too."

Tanya's mum sucked her bottom lip. "What's brought all this on?"

"It's Siobhán. She thinks she's better than me. She has an amazing brand-new dress and is doing well at the Montague Academy. She thinks she can beat me at Worlds."

"Sweetie, didn't I tell you about Siobhán? She was always jealous of you. Now you have to work hard and show her who the real champion is, isn't that right?"

Tanya nodded adamantly.

"Donegal is miles away for a feis. But maybe it would be a good idea to get you out of Dublin for a time. Let me see what I can do."

Chapter 24

Siobhán felt bad about shouting at her best friend. When she got home, she told her big sister everything. Ruth was proud of Siobhán for sticking up for herself and told her there were plenty more fish-friends in the sea.

Anna Maria was also delighted when Ruth told her that Siobhán and Tanya had fallen out. She ordered pizza to celebrate.

"And the mother, she is the worst," said Anna Maria.

"Andrea isn't always mean. She brought me to feises with Tanya and even helped me win a prelim," Siobhán protested. "And Tanya isn't so bad. Sometimes it's easier to let her get her own way."

"Andrea was only nice to you so that her poor little Tan-Wans wouldn't get lonely at the competition and make a show of herself on stage. She didn't do that to be kind to you, Siobhán," said Ruth.

Siobhán felt so upset. "I'm giving up dancing," she said glumly.

"Nonsense!" said Anna Maria. "And remember this. Sometimes you feel really sad, honey, and you didn't do anything wrong, so that's not good is it?"

Ruth chipped in. "You don't want to dance any more just because of Tanya? That's crazy, sis. Tanya always said she was better than you, and you believed it. She's afraid you're better, and you are! You love Irish dancing! Stop letting on that you don't."

Siobhán couldn't deny how much she loved performing and how much fun she had at dance class, messing around with steps.

"And you like your new dance school, don't you?"

Siobhán nodded. Ruth was right. Ruth ruffled her hair and smiled. Tanya knew she wasn't thinking clearly. She was dancing better than ever. She had to keep it up.

Chapter 25

Tanya practised really hard over the next few weeks. The Worlds were to be held in Dublin in the first week of April, and that worried Tanya. She'd heard that Siobhán was doing very well at other competitions. They hadn't faced each other competitively since the Dundrum feis.

Deep down, Tanya knew Siobhán was improving, but the fact that the Worlds were in Dublin meant she would have to see her stupid face and dance against her. Had the Worlds been abroad, Siobhán's parents wouldn't have been able to afford to go, especially after buying a new house.

Tanya and her mother agreed that the best preparation for Worlds was to compete in the Dundalk feis, the Clare feis and a few local feiseanna. The Dundalk feis was a big competition, with some of the finest dancers from all around Ulster and dancers from as far away as Limerick, but Siobhán was not one of them. Tanya danced incredibly. Her heavy jig was flawless, her slip jig graceful and her Planxty Davis perfect. She felt more relaxed on stage dancing for enjoyment, and her natural ability came to the fore. Not trying to win turned out to be a winning strategy. Tanya won all three rounds and was the Dundalk feis champion.

Tanya and Christian spent a lot of time together, playing all sorts of games. Unfortunately Christian wasn't very coordinated. He was always hurting himself because of his clumsiness. Most unfortunate was when his clumsiness had a direct effect on Tanya's well-being. Christian was pretending to be Tarzan one day when a branch he had been hanging off snapped. Tanya, standing directly underneath, became the cushion that prevented Christian from being seriously injured. Tanya was too winded to yelp, but soon she cried in agony as she felt the pain in her knee. Christian's dad carried her inside. He made some special home-made Finnish medicine that helped bring the swelling down, but

Tanya was distraught. Christian wished it had been him who had been hurt.

Tanya went to physio a few times that week. The injury wasn't serious—just a knee sprain—but it was affecting certain movements.

Christian felt so bad about what had happened he didn't come to school all week. His mother said she had never seen him so quiet. One day, he arrived at Tanya's house with a gift that he had wrapped in papier mâché. Christian couldn't look Tanya in the eye as she tried to unwrap what was clearly an Easter egg no longer in its box. Tanya smiled when she saw the gold wrapping.

"It's an Easter egg," Christian said shyly. "I saved it for a special occasion. It was my favourite one, the one I wanted to eat the most last year."

Tanya's face dropped. "From last year?"

"I hope you like it," Christian added solemnly.

"Eh, thanks. Really Christian, thank you."

Tanya's knee recovered enough for her to attend the Lucan feis. Siobhán's was the first face she saw that day in the foyer. Siobhán stopped stretching when she saw Tanya. Tanya stopped mid-stride, and the former friends stared at each other. As if in slow motion, Siobhán's face changed. Her lip started to curl ever so slightly on the right side of her face. For a moment, Tanya thought she was about to smile. Instead she squinted and a shot a spiteful glance at Tanya. Siobhán swung her head round dramatically and continued stretching.

Tanya clenched her teeth.

Andrea was pleased as she watched Tanya perfectly mark out her steps in the foyer before going on stage. Tanya danced an amazing heavy jig and gulped water afterwards with a satisfied look on her face. Siobhán danced shortly afterwards. Tanya's eyes grew large as she watched Siobhán make her way around the stage. Her soft-shoe dancing had improved so much. Tanya felt a little nervous.

The girls bumped into each other in the bathroom shortly afterwards. Nicole from Siobhán's new dance school giggled alongside Siobhán as they washed their hands.

"You'll be on the podium today if you keep it up," said Nicole.

"Looks like it," said Siobhán as she saw Tanya coming.

Tanya pulled some tissues from the dispenser and blew her nose with exaggeration. She continued blowing loudly and stared deep into Siobhán's eyes as she crumpled the tissue and threw it in the bin.

"Do you have a problem?" said Siobhán icily.

"No, no problem. You might be on the podium, sister, but you'll be looking up at me," said Tanya with a fake smile.

Tanya changed into her light shoes. She was beginning to feel powerful after her exchange with Siobhán, and she grew in confidence during her first round of dancing. She was dancing with one other girl who wasn't very good. Tanya knew the judges would give her all their attention. But this didn't make her nervous. Her second dance was going really well up until one point when she slipped. She adjusted her feet quickly and skilfully so that no one could have possibly noticed her mistake. But one thing she could not disguise was when she winced in pain. Thankfully the dance was almost at an end. She bowed, but the walk down the steps was painful. She had jarred her sore knee. She approached her mother, holding back the tears. Andrea knew immediately that there was a problem.

"How bad?" asked Andrea.

"Maybe a six or seven," said Tanya as she rooted through her dance bag. She sat on the floor and pulled helplessly at the lid of the cooling gel. She threw the container to the ground beside her and buried her face in her hands.

Andrea knelt down and quickly unscrewed the cap and rubbed the gel into Tanya's knee, stretching her leg out gently. "It's just the Lucans, dear. We can leave if you like."

"No!" said Tanya adamantly. "I'm staying and I'm going to win. I'm going to beat Siobhán."

Tanya's leg felt stiff as she went to perform her set dance. She tried to ignore the pain, but she wasn't able to execute the moves as fluently as she would have liked. She cursed her luck as she sat icing her knee and watching Siobhán dance. Tanya knew that Siobhán couldn't possibly dance the Planxty Davis well since she had only started learning it a few weeks previously.

Within thirty seconds of Siobhán starting her set dance, both Andrea and Tanya's faces fell to the floor. Siobhán looked majestic. The steps were tight, quick and graceful, yet her face was full of focus and fury. She oozed spirit as she performed not just for the judges but for all the onlookers. Andrea looked at her daughter, who stared on with hate.

"Stay there. I'll get you some more ice, love," said Andrea.

The announcer took the microphone at the side of the stage an hour later to call out the results. Andrea sat beside Tanya and held her hand while the judges' totals were read out. Tanya spotted Siobhán and her dance teacher sitting at the opposite end. They locked eyes. Tanya gritted her teeth. The announcer tapped the microphone to make sure it was working.

"In first place, number 147, Siobhán McMahon."

Tanya struggled to catch her breath. The spectators applauded. Tanya felt her mother's grip weaken. She watched Siobhán walk side stage to line up for the presentation, her face full of disbelief.

"In second place, number 164, Tanya Armstrong."

Tanya felt sick. She tried to smile as she made her way to line up next to Siobhán. When all the results were called, the winners flocked to the podium to collect their medals and trophies. Tanya found it almost impossible to maintain her smile as she stood underneath a jubilant Siobhán on the podium. Siobhán's teeth shone so bright, and she completely ignored Tanya as they came off stage. Tanya gave the trophy to Andrea, whose face was solemn.

At that moment, Anna Maria ushered Siobhán past them. "It eez the best thing ever happened my daughter. No longer can your girl bully her. I always knew she was a better girl in every way," said Anna Maria smugly.

Andrea was too stunned to reply. Her cheeks reddened as she sent Tanya off to get changed.

Chapter 26

Andrea made Tanya rest for a week until her knee felt strong again. Tanya invited Christian round to keep her company. Mrs Leonard called to tell Andrea there was some abusive behaviour reported on social media between girls at their school and girls in the Ashbourne school. Andrea banned Tanya from using the internet for a few days, even though Tanya told her it was mainly friends of Siobhán's who were saying nasty things and she hadn't responded.

The following Monday, Andrea and Tanya began practising again, but Tanya had lost all passion and motivation. Her energy was low, and she gave up far too easily.

"Can you at least try to put some oomph into it, Tans?" Andrea asked as she watched Tanya do her step about.

"Mam, I can't. I'm just not able. My leg is sore everywhere, and I can't do anything fast enough."

Andrea studied her daughter's pale features and sad face and nodded. "OK love. Let's just leave it for now. Those *steps* ... I've never been sure about them. They're too over the top for my liking."

"It's not the steps' fault, it's just my feet. Anyways, Mrs Leonard says the judges love fancy footwork."

Andrea snorted. "Whatever. Off you go, so."

Tanya felt terrible letting her mother down.

On Thursday morning, Andrea came into Tanya's bedroom and woke her up with a little shake.

"Mam, it's four in the morning."

"I know, sweetheart, but you aren't going to school today. I have a little surprise for you."

"What do you mean?"

"Get dressed. You're going to need this, by the way."

Her mother handed her a passport but wouldn't tell her where they were going. They got a taxi to the airport, and it wasn't until they were waiting at their gate that Tanya realised they were going to London.

"But why, Mam?" Tanya asked.

"I just need to get some things for a wedding I'm going to next month and didn't want to come on my own. Let's just call it a girls' weekend."

When they arrived in London, they did all sorts of lovely things like seeing the sights, having tea in the poshest hotels and eating ice cream on the banks of the Thames. Andrea bought Tanya jeans and tops and jewellery and all sorts of wonderful things. They went for a lovely dinner in a fancy five-star restaurant, which they had to get dressed up for. The biggest surprise was left until the end of the day. They headed for Kensington, and Andrea handed Tanya a ticket for a show—*StepAbout*!

Tanya had seen the show before when she was six years old and had been dying to see it again. Seeing it in the Royal Albert Hall in London would be amazing.

They had front row seats. The show was incredible. Tanya's heart raced as the finale ended.

"Did you enjoy it?" Andrea asked.

Tanya nodded, unable to say anything.

"Well, that's just a part of the surprise. You won't believe what comes next."

***

They walked towards side stage, where a big black curtain separated front of house and backstage. A security guard stood next to a crack in the curtain. He stopped Andrea, but she whispered in his ear. A few minutes later, Boris McNally, the former principal dancer and Andrea's ex-partner, came round and greeted her with a big hug.

They went back stage, and Tanya got to see all the dancers running around in their sweaty underwear, waiting to get showered and changed so they could go out and celebrate another great show. They were all laughing and shouting and in party mode. Tanya felt amazing. She wanted to be a professional dancer now more than ever.

"Tanya, do you want to meet the leading pair?" said Boris.

"Really?"

"Of course." He smiled. He led Tanya to a door at the end of the corridor. There was a giant gold star on the door with the name Scott Kingsley in bold black letters on top. Boris knocked on the door. "Scott? Can we come in a minute?"

The three walked into a huge dressing room with a large brown couch and a TV mounted on the wall. Scott Kingsley sat in a chair facing a mirror, hundreds of cotton pads in front of him as he wiped make-up from his sweaty face. He wore a raggedy old T-shirt with holes in it and faded black tracksuit bottoms. He jumped up immediately with a golden smile and went straight to Tanya.

"Is this Tanya? Hey, how's it going? I'm Scott. I heard you're a great dancer," he said in a syrupy Australian accent.

He was so tall he had to get down on one knee to make eye contact with Tanya and shake her hand.

Tanya grabbed the hem of her mother's skirt. Her face fizzled with embarrassment.

"Hello," she said timidly. She could barely speak. Scott Kingsley was even more gorgeous in real life than on the posters.

"She must like you, Scott," said Andrea. "I must have you round to our house sometime. This is the quietest I've ever seen her."

Things went from amazing to unreal shortly afterwards. Next stop was the dressing room of Fionnuala McBride—the leading lady! Fionnuala was Tanya's favourite ever dancer.

"Hi Tanya, did you enjoy the show?" Fionnuala was from County Cork and had a sing-song accent that went up and down like a kite in the wind.

"Oh my God, it was just superb," said Tanya, who had got over her shyness now.

"So your mum is going shopping for a wedding outfit tomorrow. You don't want to do that, do you?" Fionnuala asked with a friendly smile.

Tanya shook her head no.

"Well, if you want, you can hang out with me for a bit and maybe get some coffee or ice cream?"

Tanya nodded excitedly.

"And maybe then I'll let you come and do a warm up with me and the other girls before tomorrow's matinée. You think you'd like that?"

Tanya clasped her hands over her mouth, and Fionnuala gave her a big squeeze.

"Good. It's a date!"

Chapter 27

Tanya, Fionnuala McBride and another dancer called Margie Thomas went to a nice coffee shop down a little alley that reminded Tanya of something from Harry Potter. Margie was from California and had the bushiest blonde hair imaginable. She had a constant smile on her face and a really strong American accent. They walked along the riverbank, a breeze blowing their hair into their faces, and chatted about tour life while eating ice cream. Tanya even asked how much money they made. The dancers burst out laughing.

"What's the best thing about it all?" Tanya asked.

Fionnuala answered immediately. "It has to be a standing ovation and the amazing adrenaline rush you get."

Margie was quick to add. "And the boys. The boys are cute!"

The three girls laughed.

"What's your favourite thing about dancing?" Margie asked.

Tanya had to think. Only the day before, she'd hated everything about it. How long ago that seemed. "I think I love everything about it. I love how it makes me feel. Dancing is great craic. I'd love it more if everyone clapped for me, I suppose."

They made their way to the Royal Albert Hall. It was only one o'clock, but they had a matinée at four and had to be there to sign in and warm up. The dance captain called all the dancers backstage for a 20-minute cardio session. Fionnuala told Tanya to join in. It was cool to be so close to the entire dance cast. Everyone was so fit and toned and dedicated. Tanya understood now the sacrifices you have to make to become part of a professional dance team. She was determined to do the workout as well as any of the adults.

As they stretched, a long-haired man wearing overalls and boots walked by.

"I have a great idea," said Fionnuala loudly. "Tanya, do you know the steps to 'StepAbout'?"

Tanya nodded.

"That man is the sound technician."

Fionnuala organised for the engineer to dim the lights and prepare the "StepAbout" track. Then Fionnuala and Tanya danced it on stage while some of the other dancers sat in the front row watching. When Fionnuala and Tanya raised their hands to the air with the final steps, their little audience started hollering and whooping. Tanya felt amazing.

After that, Fionnuala showed her where the sound and light technicians took care of everything from a booth at the back of the theatre. Then she showed her where the costumes were kept, the cast's changing rooms and the green room.

"OK, are you ready for your dance lesson now?"

Tanya nodded. It was just the two of them in the warm-up room.

"Which set dance do you dance?"

"The Planxty Davis."

Fionnuala found a CD and played the track. Then she stood back and watched Tanya dance.

Tanya finished and took a breath. Fionnuala spun round, hit a button and the track started again. She fast forwarded through the first 40 seconds.

"OK, again, please. I'll count you in."

Tanya did as she was told. When she finished dancing, Fionnuala called her over.

"OK Tanya, that wasn't bad," she said in a serious tone. "How long have you been dancing these steps?"

"Um, a good few months," said Tanya.

"OK Tanya, I'm going to be honest with you. If you want to be a champion dancer, we need to work on some things. At first I thought I was imagining it, but when you danced a second time, I noticed some things you could work on."

Tanya's face fell.

"I know it's probably hard for you to hear, but now is a good time. If we change some things now, you could be a contender to win Worlds next year or maybe the year after."

"Next year? Not this year?"

Fionnuala shook her head. Her softness had quickly faded. "I don't think so. Your steps are too complicated, and as a result of trying to get them right, your basic technique has suffered. I'm surprised your dance teacher hasn't spotted it."

"What do you mean?"

"For starters, you are landing flat after your jumps. You need to be getting good elevation but still landing on your toes."

Tanya stared at the dusty wooden floorboards.

"I'm sorry I sound like a monster, Tanya. But I didn't win world titles and become the lead in this show from people telling me how brilliant I was. When I was your age, I had never even won a preliminary competition. I was very lucky to have an amazing dance teacher who stuck with me. Hard work is the key. Now go get a big drink of water, and we'll get to work."

Tanya practised with Fionnuala for almost a full hour and felt much better afterwards. Fionnuala gave her a kiss on the cheek and wished her well.

"You've got great ability, Tanya. Time to work hard now. Good luck! And you never know, I might see you at Worlds. I go every year for the senior ladies and senior men. If you see me, come say hi!"

Chapter 28

Tanya returned from London rejuvenated and determined. There were two weeks left before Worlds. She had taken in and believed everything Fionnuala had told her, everything except not being able to win Worlds this year.

"Fionnuala said my basic technique wasn't strong enough to dance the moves. She said they were a bit complicated," said Tanya as she tied her Capezios, sitting on the dance-room floor.

Andrea grunted. "I knew it. I knew the material Mrs Leonard was making you learn was over the top. But it's not too late. I'm going to change it slightly."

Andrea made Tanya dance all her dances and, over the course of the evening, tweaked and simplified them. Tanya worked hard to make sure she landed on her toes and kept her foot pointed at the back when lifting. The following day, her body ached so much she could hardly walk. She watched YouTube clips of other dancers as well as the Parade of Champions from last year's North American Nationals to suss out some of the girls she'd be competing against. Some were excellent. Girls called Melanie O'Connor from Chicago and Linda Drinklater from Columbus were especially good. Melanie had won the Oireachtas, and Linda was the North American national champion. They were strong, precise and beautiful. Tanya felt nervous but reminded herself that they might not make the expensive journey from the States to Ireland for a dance competition.

The girls from Ashbourne and the girls from Drumcondra were bickering on social media once more. Siobhán had promised to shut Tanya up once and for all by beating her at Worlds, and one of the girls in Tanya's school threatened to kick Siobhán if she didn't keep her mouth closed. Soon a website moderator came and threatened to ban the girls. The comments were removed, but not before the entire dance community knew what was about to take place the following week in Dublin's Hilton Hotel.

Tanya's final week of practice was very productive. Her newly tweaked slip jig and set dance flowed much better without the complicated steps. They left the hornpipe as it was. It was a difficult dance with complicated steps, but Tanya was able for it, especially with all the extra training she had been doing over the past weeks. At the end of practice, Andrea was very pleased with her daughter.

"I have one more surprise for you, dear."

"You do?" said Tanya excitedly. "But you've already done so much for me. But don't get me wrong—I love surprises, so keep 'em coming!"

"This last surprise you'll only get on the big day, OK?"

Tanya nodded excitedly.

"And you're not to give it to Christian, you hear me?" said Andrea.

Chapter 29

Before they packed the car to go to Worlds, Andrea called Tanya into her bedroom. She made Tanya close her eyes and sat her on the bed. When she opened them, there was the most amazing gold dance dress laid out on the bed beside her. Tanya's eyes lit up.

"Gold because you're a winner, my dear," said Andrea.

"And you were afraid I might give this to Christian?" smiled Tanya. "How did you know what size to get?"

"I measured you in your sleep," Andrea joked.

Tanya hugged her mam tightly.

That Sunday, Andrea and Tanya arrived at the Hilton Hotel full of confidence and energy. They had invited Christian along because he had begged and begged to see "The world's best ever magic dancer with super feet in the entire universe".

Tanya was dancing on Monday. She woke fresh that morning. While eating breakfast, she thought back to the time she got nervous without Siobhán before feiseanna and thought how silly she was.

She saw Siobhán in the lobby of the hotel warming up by herself. Tanya skipped for five minutes and danced all three of her dances in her socks as a light warm-up. The foyer was incredibly busy with people moving between the two large functions rooms where the dancing competitions were taking place. Tanya found a quiet part and sat against a wall cross-legged. She closed her eyes and slowed her breathing. She tried to block out all the noise—the noise in the hall and the noise in her brain. She then visualised herself dancing her steps, dancing with a great big smile on her face. After a couple of minutes of relaxation, she felt ready. She got changed and prepared for the big day.

Siobhán and Tanya stood next to each other as they waited to dance. Tanya was in the group immediately before Siobhán.

All Tanya's hard work and commitment would go into a couple of minutes of dancing, but she tried not to think about that. She tried to picture Grandad Dermot's pretend-angry face. She stared at all the judges and pretended they were clowns there for a kiddie's party. She held her breath as the opening bars played. The bright lights shone off her golden twinkly dress, making her feel like a star. Tanya skipped around stage effortlessly, hammering beats with great precision and perfect timing. The air swooshed around her legs as she spun and took flight, sailing across stage, rocking and crisscrossing with the sharpness of a fencing champion. It couldn't have gone any better.

Tanya was shocked to see Fionnuala McBride greet her as she came off stage.

"Wow Tanya, that was really great," she said, almost singing.

"Thanks," said Tanya, who stood to the side panting.

"Do you want to get a drink?"

"Yes, in a minute. I just have to watch this girl first." She nodded towards Siobhán.

"Is she your friend?"

Tanya shook her head dramatically. "No. Well, she used to be."

They were quiet for a moment as the dancing commenced.

Siobhán danced well, showing off some lovely footwork with her loose ankles.

"She's doing a good job," Fionnuala whispered.

But all of a sudden, after doing a high kick, Siobhán's foot went from under her, and she landed with a thud on her bottom. She was back on her feet lightning fast and continued dancing perfectly.

Tanya clasped her hand to her mouth, confused. She noticed two of the judges mark their cards, deducting points in all probability.

"Oh dear," said Fionnuala.

"Will she lose because of that?"

"She could do," said Fionnuala sadly

When the dance ended, Fionnuala picked up where they had left off. "So why isn't she your friend anymore?"

"She ditched me and moved to another dance school," said Tanya

"That's a shame. But why aren't you friends?"

"Because she thinks she's better than me."

"That's silly," said Fionnuala with a sad smile.

"I suppose."

"It's not worth falling out over competitions. And it's never good to be jealous. You should say hard luck to her."

"I have to go find my mam," said Tanya

Andrea had an evil grin on her face.

"Did you see that? Serves her right."

"Mam, that's mean. Siobhán is still a nice person."

"You want to beat her, don't you?" said Andrea.

"Yes. But I want to beat her because I'm a better dancer, not because she fell."

Andrea pursed her lips.

Chapter 30

There was quite a buzz in the foyer as word went round about how well two American dancers were performing. An English girl called Susan Dartmouth was said to have danced brilliantly, although when Tanya asked the girls from her dance school if they had seen her, none of them had.

"I heard she was out of this world."

"Apparently it was like she was floating," said another.

Christian and Tanya went to get a bar of chocolate while they waited for Tanya's next dance. Siobhán was in the queue in front of her. Tanya didn't want to speak to her, but an English girl standing beside her said something to Siobhán, and Tanya overheard.

"Too bad about your slip. I saw the dance. You were doing really well, but looks like your chances are gone now. Still, maybe you'll get on the podium."

Siobhán bowed her head. As she turned away with her sweets, she caught Tanya's eye. Tanya saw how tearful Siobhán was and felt bad for her.

Tanya glowed with the confidence she had gained from her flawless heavy shoe as she went to dance her slip jig. She danced it brilliantly, hitting all her double clicks and high clicks. She nailed her double axels and made sure to keep her left foot turned out at the back. But as she spun and headed towards stage left, the other girl unexpectedly crossed her path. The two girls brushed lightly, which caused Tanya to mix up her feet and lose her composure. Tanya's face was red with fury, but she finished her dance strongly. She felt a twinge in her ankle as she came off stage and iced it immediately.

"Let's find that number 187 girl and kill her," said Christian with a grin as he sauntered over. Tanya would have loved to.

Siobhán spotted her and gave a sad smile. Tanya stayed to watch Siobhán's light shoe. The reality was that Siobhán probably couldn't win the championship now, so the pressure was off her. She floated across stage with amazing charisma, as if she owned the floor.

Next on stage was Melanie O'Connor from Chicago. Her dance was solid but not spectacular. Shortly afterwards, it was Linda Drinklater's turn. She executed her complicated steps perfectly. There seemed to be an extra burst of applause and excited whispers as she took her bow. Tanya's stomach felt heavy, like an anchor had been dropped. Christian's face was flushed.

"Wow, that was awesome. She has the fastest feet on the planet!"

Tanya's face dropped. She knew that Christian might well be right.

Chapter 31

Everyone waited in the hall for the recalls to be announced. Tanya wondered if Siobhán would get a recall after slipping and became nervous that she might not get one herself after almost bumping into the girl in her last dance. When their numbers were called, Tanya caught Siobhán's eye, and they shared a half-smile.

The dancers had some time off before the recalls. Tanya walked gingerly outside, her ankle slightly numb from all the ice. Christian had disappeared, and she had to find him. She heard a tremendous racket as she passed the girls' toilets. She went in to have a look and saw Christian frightened for his life with three girls standing around him menacingly.

"Hey Lankenstein, get the heck out of the girls' bathroom, you weirdo. I'll report you to the police, and I'll kick you where the sun don't shine so you can never walk again," said Linda Drinklater in her American accent. Christian stood stiff, his face matching the white-tiled walls. He had paper and pen in his hand.

"But I was just looking for an autograph," he yelped.

Linda Drinklater and her two friends edged closer, fists raised. Just as Tanya was about to run over to intervene, Siobhán came out of a cubicle, ran across and shoved all the girls out of Christian's way and took him by the hand.

"Leave him alone," she shouted to the crowd of girls. "He's my friend. It was just an accident, wasn't it, Christian?"

"No, not really. I saw the girl who is the best go this way and I wanted to get her auto—"

"Just a terrible misunderstanding," Siobhán said loudly, interrupting him.

"Get your creep friend outta here!" said Linda.

Tanya pushed her way through the girls, and Christian's eyes lit up as he saw her.

"Thanks, Siobhán," said Tanya, and she ushered Christian outside.

"I didn't mean to be a girl in the girls' bathroom," Christian protested. "I just saw my one and only opportunity to meet a real-life champion. But now they all just want revenge. They want to kill me."

Tanya couldn't help but laugh. She sat Christian down on a wall and told him everything would be all right.

"You know, Christian, the sign above the door, the picture of the woman in the dress, that means girls' bathroom. Boys aren't allowed in there."

"Really? I just thought it meant woman's office. I even knocked before I entered."

"Oh Christian!" said Tanya.

Soon it would be time for the set dances.

Mrs Leonard and Andrea took Tanya to the practice floor in the foyer.

"Let's get this absolutely perfect," said Mrs Leonard. "The American girl will no doubt have something special, so you have to bring your A game."

Andrea nodded in agreement. Siobhán and Anna Maria stood next to Christian, who had somehow managed to start chatting to Fionnuala McBride.

"Come on, come on Tanya. On your toes! Come on, get up!" said Mrs Leonard.

Tanya winced as her ankle began to hurt more and more. People had stopped to watch as Mrs Leonard's angry shouting increased in volume.

Tanya stopped abruptly. "I just need a minute. My foot hurts."

"Nonsense. You have to dance through the pain. The Leonard school produces winners. You can win this," Mrs Leonard said.

Tanya looked towards her mam. Andrea looked confused.

"Again. And five, six, seven, eight," shouted Mrs Leonard.

But Tanya didn't dance. She saw Siobhán and Christian and Anna Maria all looking at her. And then she saw Fionnuala McBride. Tanya gritted her teeth. She counted herself in.

"And five, six, seven, eight." Mrs Leonard hummed the tune, and Tanya tried to ignore the pain and dance as hard as she could. But soon the pain was too much. She wasn't able to perform any of the moves properly and tears ran down her cheeks as she continued trying.

"STOP!" a voice shouted. It was Anna Maria.

Tanya collapsed, holding her ankle. Siobhán ran to her side and hugged her.

"This is crazy. The girl can no dance. She is injured," said Anna Maria.

"She can dance. She can win this," said Mrs Leonard.

Fionnuala joined the discussion. "She physically can't dance. Look at her."

"She is just a little girl. She is only eleven. She can do again next year and the other years," said Anna Maria.

Andrea looked icily at Anna Maria and Fionnuala.

"She'll be fine in a minute," said Mrs Leonard, who went over to help Tanya to her feet.

Andrea fumed. "Leave her," she shouted. "Tanya, are you OK?"

Siobhán released Tanya from their embrace. Tanya looked around at the audience. She shook her head slowly.

Andrea turned to Mrs Leonard. "It's not about winning. It's about being happy. I'm taking her home." Andrea knelt by her daughter's side. "I'm so sorry I pushed you too hard and only cared about winning. The truth is, when I was lead in *StepAbout*, I thought I was invincible. I stopped working as hard. Then I got injured, and I was off for two months, and when I came back, I thought I'd be lead again. But they promoted another girl in my place, and no matter how hard I worked, I didn't get to dance lead again. I guess I just didn't want you to learn things the hard way. I'm sorry. You should dance for fun."

Tanya hugged her mother and cried.

"I have such a headache. We should get straight out of here. Don't worry about changing." Andrea stood up and walked towards Anna Maria. "I'm sorry, Anna Maria, about everything that's gone on before."

Anna Maria smiled gently. "No problem. You know, if you want, Tanya can stay, if she wants. I can bring her home."

Andrea looked at her daughter.

Tanya looked across to Siobhán. "What do you think, Siobhán?"

Siobhán smiled excitedly.

***

Anna Maria located a pair of crutches for Tanya and brought Christian with her to get some tea. Tanya sat in the hall icing her foot as Miss Montague gave Siobhán some last words of advice before her set dance.

"I'm really sorry about everything that's happened," said Siobhán before she lined up to dance.

"Me too. I'm sorry I was such a baby. I'm so sorry I blamed you for my losing streak and for making you feel bad for moving away. And for always thinking I was better than you."

"I forgive you."

"I really missed you, you know."

Siobhán grinned. "I knew you would."

"Thanks for sticking up for Christian earlier," said Tanya.

"Poor Christian. Those girls are so horrible and nasty," said Siobhán. "I better go now."

"Show them who's boss," said Tanya.

Siobhán looked fierce as she waited for the music to start. She had amazing presence on stage for such a small girl, her olive skin and pretty face shining into the audience. She delivered all her moves so stylishly, setting them up slowly and delivering wonderfully intricate footwork. Tanya looked on in admiration, goose bumps on her legs. Siobhán continued to roll out the precise moves. Everything looked natural and effortless. Tanya noticed that one of the judges had taken his glasses off, put his pen down and folded his arms to fully concentrate on the dance. There was a large cheer as Siobhán bowed.

When Siobhán arrived back to where they were sitting, she was panting. She hugged her mother and high-fived Tanya.

"I'm speechless," said Tanya.

Chapter 32

Siobhán and Tanya held hands as the scoreboard lit up and the announcer began calling out the judges' results. Tanya was disappointed her number wasn't up there, but she tried not to look sad and ruin the excitement for Siobhán. Siobhán must have noticed.

"Don't worry, Tans. You'll be back next year, stronger than ever."

When the final judge's results appeared on the board, there was a loud cheer from the opposite end of the hall. Tanya stood on one leg to see. All she could see was an American flag and lots of people hugging. She then turned to Siobhán, who was counting on her fingers.

She looked across at Tanya with an anxious face. "Aw God, Tanya, I wish I was good at maths. I'm too nervous to add."

"Here, let me," Tanya quickly totted up her scores. After a quick scan of the scoreboard, she said, "You've done well, Shivs, but I can't be sure how well."

The girls stopped talking as the announcer called the winner to the stage. It was Linda Drinklater. Christian clapped long and loud.

Tanya elbowed him. "Hey, she was mean to you!"

"Yes, but she's the bestest dancing magician girl I've ever seen."

Both Tanya and Siobhán watched with envious eyes as Linda put on her sash and stood on the podium waving her trophy. The runners-up were called one by one.

"This year's tenth place is number 234, Siobhán McMahon."

Siobhán was too stunned to celebrate. Anna Maria kissed her on the cheek, and Tanya gave her a big hug.

She joined the other winners on stage and blew kisses towards Tanya, Christian and her mam. Tanya's chest was crushed with pride.

She heard Christian sniffling. "I'm so proud right now, I could just die," he said.

"Me too, Christian, me too."

Seán de Gallai

About The Author

This is Seán de Gallai's second book and first Middle Grade novel. He is also the author of *The Dancer. Steps From The Dark* – a novel for Young Adults. He spends half his time teaching in a primary school in Dublin and the other half writing books in Donegal.

www.seandegallai.com

Seán de Gallai

Step Sisters

88875844R00128

Made in the USA
Middletown, DE
13 September 2018